Bold
as Brass

Bold
as Brass

Bettejane Synott Wesson

Library of Congress Control Number: 2013908057
ISBN: Hardcover   978-1-4836-3590-3
                Softcover   978-1-4836-3589-7
                Ebook   978-1-4836-3591-0

This book was printed in the United States of America.

Rev. date: 05/02/2013

To order additional copies of this book, contact:
Xlibris Corporation
1-888-795-4274
www.Xlibris.com
Orders@Xlibris.com
128616

CONTENTS

Introduction 9

Buckingham Palace.. 13

Picturing The Dead 21

Scovill's Dam 27

Saturday Night Swells.. 35

In The Garden 43

Riverside 51

The Rich Are Different... 59

Little Dolls 69

Ah, Fresh Air 75

Dodo 83

Father Dooley's Cottage 91

Yankee Doodle Dandy 99

Going Places.. 107

My Name Is Ted 117

The End Of The Line... 125

Time Goes By 133

What I Learned From Reading Fannie Hurst 141

Dancing On The Moon 151

Doll Cake 161

Glads.. 169

Vanity 175

Advantage 185

Ghost Stories 193

Jingle Bells... 201

To Betty.
After you, they broke the mold.

INTRODUCTION

The twenty-four stories told in *Bold as Brass* are fiction, though they are inspired by my own history, an Irish Catholic one, in my hometown of Waterbury, Connecticut.

My stories begin with "Buckingham Palace," based on something my grandfather often said about my mother. I imagined a scene where a young Betty might have overheard this statement and believed it to be true.

The more I thought about my mother, the more stories I remembered. And as I wrote them down, I felt that I was coming to know her not just as my mother but also as my friend. I began to think of those stories as "Betty" stories. And when I came across the exuberant photo of her that I've used for this book's cover, I knew at once that the title of my book should be *Bold as Brass*, an expression used about Betty in "Buckingham Palace."

The places in the Waterbury area stories are real, of course, and some of the incidents may have actually happened to someone, somewhere, but for sure not in the ways I've imagined them or to the characters whom I have created.

You might think that you recognize a person or two. But that is not possible, because all my characters are invented, with the exception of my immediate family, whose stories I have borrowed and told from my own perspective.

My mother and father, my grandparents, and my little sister have all given me permission from heaven to tell their stories, and for me, they have lived again as I wrote this book.

It goes without saying that the incomparable Betty, Rob, Cora and Mike, Zora and Donal, and especially little Molly will always be alive in my heart.

BUCKINGHAM PALACE

Betty is dreaming as she walks, dreaming with open eyes. Behind her, as she climbs Walnut Street, lies Saint Mary's School, a dark, red brick fortress with a witchy mansard roof. Along her uphill route, triple-decker houses loom on either side. Some have shingled turrets. Many have a stained-glass windowpane in their front door or an oriel window set to one side. All have wide front porches that decrease in size as they rise from the first floor to the second and the third. These are the houses of the workers of Waterbury, Connecticut—the Brass Capital of the World. Betty lives in one of them. She imagines the houses as castles.

It is 1932. The brass mills are working full tilt. Her dad and all his siblings here in America, a sister and two brothers, have come from Killarney to work at Scovill's Brass. Betty's mother, though, to their way of thinking, does not work. Rising before the first light of dawn while the others are still warm in their beds, she begins breakfast preparations for the household. Each day, including Sunday, the acknowledged day of rest, continues her endless domestic cycle of washing, cooking, ironing, and tidying the house. Betty is walking home from school to help her mother with dinner, which is what the workers call the meal they eat each day at noon.

The streets that lead to her home have romantic names: Cherry, Violet, Drake. Betty reads them out loud to her brother Pat, who trails her, dragging a stick. Pat is six. She is eight. Toys are nonexistent in the

Keane household, so it is Betty's imagination that makes the fun for the two of them.

"Mam! Where are the forks?" Betty calls as she enters the dining room. They could be anywhere. Housekeeping is not Mrs. Keane's forte. Betty finds them in the laundry basket and sets them out alongside the assortment of cups and plates from the stack in the pantry. Among the plain white ones and a few with green borders are two with a transfer pattern of roses at their centers. Pat is under the table, pretending the tablecloth is a tent.

"When I'm grown, I'll have dishes that match," she tells him. "Beautiful ones. And a pony too. For you," she adds as an afterthought.

"Oh, can it be a gray one?" Pat asks. He covets the dapple-gray rocking horse of the boy next door.

"Sure, Pat," says Betty. "Why not?"

Fresh in Betty's mind is last night's conversation with her mother. Sometimes when it's just the two of them at the kitchen sink, washing the supper dishes, Mam tells stories about what life was like in Ireland when she was a girl.

Mam's house there has a name, Dinis. It means "island of dark water." The house's island is on Killarney's Middle Lake, just beyond the old weir bridge that tourists pass under on their way to Dinis for tea. The tourists arrive in wooden boats painted in bright primary colors and rowed by a team of boatmen. Mam's tales of her childhood, of the dressmaker who came twice a year to make her new clothes and the big wooden dollhouse that was a favored plaything, are unimaginable to Betty, a world of things she has never seen. The story she likes best, and asks to hear over and over, is of a tourist woman who boldly used the diamond in her ring to scratch her initials in the tearoom's windowpane. If she went there to Dinis, Betty tells herself, the first thing she would do is to make a beeline to that window and scratch her own name on it, at the very top.

Each morning, Betty's mother pins a round silver brooch to her cotton housedress. Its features—a conical stone tower, an Irish wolfhound and a harp—are wreathed in a border of shamrocks. The pin is called a Tara brooch. Betty's own grandfather created this one's unique design, which seems to her to hint at an untold story that she would like to hear.

"There were only two of these fashioned," Mam has explained. "One for my sister Una and one for me."

Betty often pictures this aunt, whom she has never met, on the other side of the world, pinning her brooch to her dress, the two ornaments complimenting each other like those matching dishes she plans to have one day.

"Do you and Aunt Una pin them to your nightgowns as well?" she asks.

"Don't be bold," her mother replies. "A bold child will never have a day's luck."

"Do you ever wish you could go back there?" Betty continues.

Taking the potatoes from the oven, Zora hesitates for a moment, then explains, "My father was a hard man. You'd have as much luck whistling jigs to a milestone as trying to change his mind once it was made up. If I'd returned home, I'd not have been able to take you with me. He said as much when I wrote to him and asked."

Betty cannot understand why her mother left in the first place if Ireland was so swell, but details have proved impossible to dig out of Zora. The responsibility for keeping her mother anchored here in Waterbury's north end is a weight she carries. Betty might feel less obligated if she felt that she belonged here too. But she is the blue-eyed dreamer in a family of hazel-eyed, hardworking kin.

"Ladies! Where is the laundry?" Aunt Dolly demands in the sharp tone she uses whenever Betty's father is out of sight. She is suddenly there, framed in the kitchen doorway, elbows on her hips. She is Dad's little sister and the only one of three who has dared to come and live in America.

"I need my white blouse for tonight," she tells them. The clothes, sheets, and towels must all be washed by hand and then boiled on the stove, with stubborn spots given extra attention on the wooden scrub board. Although they exist in 1932, no washing machine sits in the Keane household's kitchen. An assortment of shirts and sheets are pegged out on the clothesline in the backyard. Two more baskets wait their turn beneath the legs of the porcelain sink.

"Herself has the life of Riley here and little enough to do all day while we're off to Scovill's with the morning whistle," Aunt Dolly often complains to Uncle Jimmy of Zora. She always adds, "I'd be only too glad to sit here at home myself like the queen if I had the chance."

The queen, Betty knows, lives in England, at Buckingham Palace. Betty herself was born close by in Wales while her parents were en route to America.

"We're Celtic thoroughbreds," Dad has often remarked. "We've the blood of kings. Sure, we Irish are a noble race." His statement squares with Mam's tales of paradise lost but not with his, which include seven children and two parents crammed into a three-room cottage on the estate where they worked as gardeners and maids. Dad's other sisters and one little brother have remained in Ireland.

"And are likely to stay there, thank God," Betty has heard Mam tell their landlady, adding, "I'm as happy as if I'd been crowned queen now that they've given up emigrating. The streets of Killarney must be nearly deserted with the lot of them under this roof on Walnut Street."

Betty shares Mam's taste for keeping her best thoughts private. It's a way of having something just for yourself in a house that more times than not feels as open as a goldfish bowl. The landlady has often remarked to Betty that Mam, who would never go out to the store without her hat and white gloves, is a lady. To Betty's mind, this is proof of her mother's elevated status. Yet if being a lady means that you have to let people walk all over you as Mam does with Dad's siblings, then Betty knows for sure that a lady is something she'll never be, though she also knows better than to ever voice that observation out loud.

Is she like her father instead? She wonders. Warm and generous with a wicked sense of humor, Donal is given to sentimentality and tears. He is as open as his wife is closed. Betty cannot imagine what drew them to each other in the first place. But these days, they maintain a polite reserve, like planets held in each other's orbits by cosmic force.

Another puzzle to Betty is the date of her parents' wedding anniversary. It's in the same month as her own birthday, but it is never celebrated. Once, Betty found a paper in Mam's top bureau drawer, the off-limits drawer. It read, Certificate of Marriage. It was dated just weeks before the date of her own birth. She knows this must be a mistake, as babies take far longer than that to produce. But she can't ask anyone in the family because that would be a dead giveaway that she'd been snooping.

Aunt Dolly is always going on about snooping. In the bedroom she shares with Betty, she is ever vigilant. She and Betty have constant battles, and when Betty wins, Dolly takes it out on her in little, painful ways like braiding her hair too tight.

"Don't put your sticky hands on my pony-skin jacket! Keep your mitts out of my candy box! Keep your eyes to yourself!"

Except for the candy, none of her admonitions are truly necessary. The candy, however, is a five-pound box of Whitman's Sampler, given to Aunt Dolly each month by the policeman who is courting her. And Betty covets the dark chocolate ones, the ones with the jelly centers.

"You're an old meanie," Betty says to her aunt. "I'll tell Dad. I'll even tell your beau what you're really like!"

"And as for you, miss, you are a bold stump. In fact, you are as bold as brass!" says Dolly with a sneer.

Oddly enough, Betty takes this as a compliment. The whole city of Waterbury is filled with things made from the gleaming yellow metal: City Hall's doors, the grilles of the banks, even the doorknobs of their rent as well as the safety pins holding up the hem of Betty's dress, all are brass.

"I'm proud to be bold," she returns. "It means I can stick up for myself!"

But it is time for dinner, and peace reigns for the moment. Betty hums as she carries the potatoes out of the kitchen to the dining room table. It's the tune of her favorite song, and she learned it from one of Uncle Dan's gramophone records. The song is called "Brian O'Lynn." It's the tale of a happy-go-lucky man of great misfortune who nonetheless persists in seeing the bright side of things. The chorus to each of the dozens of verses is always the same:

It will do!
Yes! It will do!
Said Brian O'Lynn,
It will do!

Brian O'Lynn's good nature reminds Betty of her dad, whose humor can always soften her disappointments with a well-placed quip.

"Dinner's ready," Betty calls. The family take their places at the dinner table.

"When I grow up," Betty tells them, "I'm going to have dishes that match. Beautiful ones with crimson roses and golden rims. There'll be a dapple-gray pony too," she adds with a nod to her brother, who grins.

"Well, miss. Don't you think that you are the cat's meow?" Aunt Dolly jeers. Giving her a jab with her elbow, she continues, "We'll need to be calling the *Waterbury Republican* to nominate you for Miss Paddy First 1932, I'd say."

"Leave her be, Dolly," Dad replies. "What harm is there in dreaming?"

Dad always sticks up for her. Betty pokes her tongue out at her aunt when he turns away to pass the turnips.

"Bold," her aunt mouths, with a gesture that means "I'll get you later."

Uncle Dan spears a potato with his fork. Betty serves her brother then herself. She watches out for Pat, even though he is her mother's favorite. Zora calls him the image of her favorite brother, who lives in London. Mam never hears a word from him, and Betty cannot see why this resemblance should count in Pat's favor. On the other hand, Betty resembles her father, and being his favorite often works to her advantage in the busy household.

"Grab onto a piece of bread, Pat," she says in a manner she feels is refined. Buttering it for him, she adds, "When I'm grown up, I'll have a nursemaid for my baby. And a big white house. And a maid to wash our dishes. I'll ask her to wash Mam's dishes too. In fact, I'll live the way Mam used to before she had to marry Dad and leave Ireland."

This remark stops all conversation. Donal looks up sharply at his wife. But she won't meet his eyes. The rest of the family stares at Betty with a mixture of annoyance and surprise.

"Little pitchers have big ears," Uncle Jimmy tells Aunt Dolly, who nods as if nothing out of line that Betty can ever do will surprise her.

"And the two of you could be catching flies with your mouths agape like that," Dad adds sharply. "Betty," he continues in a softer tone, "go into the kitchen like a good girl, and get your brother a glass of milk."

Betty pushes the door open and goes to the icebox. Even from the next room, she can hear her father's sigh.

"I'm thinking that it's for sure now that the stork dropped the wrong baby at Buckingham Palace the night that she was born. And what is there to be done about it? It will be uphill work for the likes of us rearing royalty in Waterbury, I'll tell you."

The milk forgotten, Betty stands transfixed by the open icebox door. There has been a mistake made, and it is a terrible one, a story of two baby girls switched by a careless bird on the dark night of their birth in the coal mining town of Burryport, Wales. Betty thinks back to all the times that Mam has urged her, "Hold your head up. You've the same name and birthday as Princess Elizabeth in England."

"I might have known," she murmurs. "The clues were in front of me all the time."

Surely, now that the cat is out of the bag, she thinks, word will be sent to Buckingham Palace as soon as possible about the mix up, and the situation put to rights.

Smoothing her cotton dress, Betty tidies her hair in the mirror above the kitchen sink. Pausing only to shine the tips of her scuffed brown oxfords on the backs of her white ankle socks, she pours Pat's milk and kicks open the door to the dining room.

"Here you go," she tells him in her most dignified voice, taking care to place the glass in front of him without her usual thump.

Spreading her skirt wide, Betty takes her seat. And as if mindful of keeping her crown upright, she inclines her head toward him and waits graciously, hands folded in her lap, to receive his thanks.

PICTURING THE DEAD

There are pictures in Betty's parlor, three sepia-toned photos of men who have posed for the photographer in their Sunday best. The pictures have always been there, or so it seems. They have become part of the furnishings of the house on Cossett Street, as much as the Victrola or the lamp with its green silk shade.

The faces have watched over the family for as far back as Betty can remember, and she is ten. Usually on a summer day, she is outside, jumping rope with her girl friends, but today has brought rain. And so, with no hope that it will end any time soon, she goes looking for her mother. A story, she thinks, will make the day go by faster.

Mrs. Keane is in the kitchen, a usual place, making soda bread.

"Add a lot of currants, Mam," Betty says, taking a handful for herself. Mrs. Keane is at the kneading part of her project, thumping the dough with her fists, then patting it into a round loaf that will go into a hot oven and come out ready for tea.

"Who are the people in our photographs?" Betty asks. "And who is Uncle Steve?" In Irish families, at least in theirs, older cousins and even sometimes family friends are referred to as uncle or aunt. It's done as a courtesy, and a mark of respect for their greater age. This works for the grown-ups who know the family lineup but not for children, who find it heavy sledding to figure out the connections.

Zora wipes her hands, puts the mixing pans into the sink to soak, and pauses.

"Steve was a lovely man. And he died too young." She explains that he was actually Betty's cousin and a son of the folks with whom Zora and her husband, Donal, and baby Betty herself stayed when they first came to America. Betty settles in at the table, all ears for a story.

"Steve had a ukulele," Zora begins, "the first I'd ever seen." This is amazing news to Betty, that an exotic instrument from an island she has only heard about at school in geography could have traveled all the way to Waterbury from Hawaii. Betty has studied the candid photo of Steve, a young man in a dark suit and tie, his white shirt stiff and shiny with starch, standing with one foot on the bottom step of the front porch, his right hand clutching the railing. From the vest pocket of his suit a watch chain glitters, but there is no trace of the exotic musical instrument he is said to have played.

"That photo was taken at Steve's graduation from Crosby High School, the year before he died," Betty's mother explains. "He'd had the loan of his father's pocket watch for the occasion. Steve's brother Jimmy had a brand-new Kodak Brownie box camera, and we all posed for pictures on the front lawn. It was a happy day."

"But where is he now, Mam?"

"He'd taken a job with a road crew after graduation, thinking he might save up for college. But one day, there was an accident. We were glad that the hospital he was taken to was Saint Mary's, because his sister was in training there to be a nurse. And sure, a broken leg can easily be fixed. But somehow Steve got a blood clot. And that was the end of him."

The suddenness of her cousin's demise shocks Betty. The idea that you can be smiling in the morning and gone by afternoon seems very wrong.

"Why would God let that happen?" she asks. Betty has been laboring over the *Baltimore Catechism* at Saint Mary's School, and the belief that good things happen to good people is freshly planted in her mind.

"Steve's father called it God's will. He told us that God did not want only old people in heaven, he had a need for young people and little children too."

Somehow Zora's explanation makes Betty feel even worse. To her, it sounds as if God is stocking a heavenly grocery store with souls of all varieties.

"Steve's wake was in their house," Zora continues. "For three days and two nights, the casket sat in the parlor. There was a black wreath on the front door, and the family dressed in black. The neighbors brought in food, and the men sat up all night with the body. No one could get any sleep with the talking. No one could sleep anyway because of his mother's crying."

Zora is silent for a bit, then continues,

"Can you imagine, his mother had bought a radio for him as a surprise for when he was to come home with his cast? An Atwater Kent radio it was, delivered the very morning that the phone call came that he had passed. His poor mother could not abide the sight of it then. So your cousin Jimmy returned it. And that was the end of radios in their house for many years."

Betty knows that Saint Joseph's Cemetery is where Steve is buried and that he took his last ride there in a long black hearse from Bergin's Funeral Home. She surmises that funeral parlors provide the black arm bands that men in the family sport on the upper left arms of their jackets when a relative dies. She's seen it done at the neighbor's next door, the black cotton strips pinned or sewed on by the woman of the house while the men smoke their cigarettes and wait.

Outside, the rain is making a little lake in their backyard.

"If we had a boat, Mam, we could go rowing," she says, pointing out the puddle that has marooned their clothesline.

"The lake I lived on when I was a girl is where my father died," Zora tells her. "A boatload of tourists had come down from the Gap of Dunloe, but one fool leaned over too far and capsized the boat. My father saw it happen from the dock and dove in. He pulled one man to shore and rescued him, but it was too much for his heart. He died at eighty-four."

Betty has studied her grandfather's photo on the bookcase. A white-bearded man in a top hat, he is posed dressed to the nines in front of his house. She has often heard the story of how her grandfather would not accept Mam's marriage. The thrilling part, in Betty's eyes, has always been the part where he'd rushed in his carriage to the train station to try and thwart the couple's escape. Their flight accounts for Betty's birthplace, Wales, where Dad had gotten work in a coal mine. Betty has grave doubts that she'd have liked Killarney. And for sure, from what she's been told of it, she would have liked a Welsh mining town even less. She feels sure that Waterbury has both of these options beat by a mile.

"Did you cry when you heard that your father was dead?" Betty asks. Though she knows better than to say it out loud, Betty privately thinks of her grandfather as a monster. And so she is surprised to hear her mother answer yes.

"The news arrived by telegram," Zora reminisces. "A letter followed, with a little holy card inside, from the funeral Mass." The card is in Zora's Sunday missal, its black edges surrounding a prayer crowned by a heart wrapped in thorns and shooting flames from its top. On the back of the card is a blurry photo about the size of a thumbnail.

A more comforting holy card is that of Zora's brother Dennis. The photo on that one is the same as the one in their parlor. Dennis smiles out at them, a sprig of holly in the lapel of his tweed jacket. His death from septic pneumonia following the influenza pandemic of 1918 is one Betty has heard before and relishes because of the spooky details.

"Tell me again about Dennis," Betty asks.

"When he took sick, he was put into the tiny bedroom off our kitchen so we women could nurse him," Zora begins. "The doctor was called. But to no avail. As he died, shoes were flung out of the bedroom, and plates fell from the kitchen shelves. I saw it for myself. Father Horgan came to give him last rites and comfort his spirit on its way to heaven. The house was blessed and all of us as well."

"But what made the shoes and plates fly?" Betty asks, as she asks every time the story is told. She is hungry for more information about what her teacher Sister Ignatius calls the next life. But Zora's enigmatic answer is always exactly the same.

"There are things beyond what humankind can know."

Betty has had the dead on her mind a lot lately. They worry her. Her catechism class has reached a chapter called "Life Everlasting." The Last Judgment is illustrated with a drawing of bodies fitted out in what looked like white sheets. In this picture, the bodies have come out of their graves and are flying through the air on their way to heaven, which is illustrated by an ornate gate with enormous rays of light set among fluffy clouds.

Betty wonders about what the dead do when they get there, if they think of us back on earth, and perhaps glance down from time to time through heaven's floor.

"Mam," she begins. "Do you think they know each other now?"

"Who?" Zora replies.

"Steve and Dennis, Mam. Do you think they met in heaven?" Betty pictures the two young men so close in age when they died, sitting down together and trading stories over a cup of tea.

"That is something we will not know until we go there ourselves," Zora says, taking the bread from the oven with the folded up dish towels she is using as potholders.

"I wonder which is sadder, Mam? Being there when a person dies or hearing about it after it is over."

"No matter how it happens, Betty, it's a hard thing to bear."

Betty tries to imagine a real person close to her, Mam for example, gone forever.

"If you or Dad died, all I'd have left would be your picture," she says.

"That's the way of it," Zora agrees. "All we have in the end are our memories, the pictures in our minds."

The kitchen door opens, and Betty's father comes in with her brother, Pat, and their dog, Lady, who announces her arrival with a bark.

"Mind the floor with your muddy shoes," Zora warns them. Donal comes around the side of the table to pick Betty up and swing her in the air, a game they both enjoy.

"We have soda bread for tea," she tells him.

"I smelled it myself all the way from East Main Street," he jokes, a feat they all know is impossible. "Let's sit down and have ourselves a feed."

"Mam was telling me stories about the men in our pictures," Betty tells him.

"Yes," Donal replies. "And with them passed on, it's for sure now that we have friends in high places."

"Don't be blasphemous," Zora warns him, pouring the tea. And to Betty, "Don't pay heed to your father's silliness."

But Donal's flippant remark has allayed Betty's fears. It's taken the idea of eternity and cut it down to size. She tells herself that she will always remember this afternoon with all four of them in the kitchen, the rain drumming against the windows, Lady asleep in her dog bed next to the stove.

The dead are at home too, in heaven, she thinks, going about their business. Perhaps they will pause a moment to look in on their kin on Cossett Street. All her family is connected by their stories, Betty sees, all the way back to Ireland and even if they have never actually met.

It's a lovely connection, she thinks, and one she is glad to have, even if it is as faint as the little telephones she and her brother Pat have recently fashioned from two empty tin cans and a length of string.

Scovill's Dam

For most of the year, Scovill's Dam lives quietly. Fed by the Mad River and a series of reservoirs in the town of Wolcott, its surrounding pine trees provide the backdrop for the changes of their deciduous companions, stands of maples that turn orange and red, go bare, and return at last to pale green.

But summer tells a different story. That's when the employees of Scovill's Brass factory and all their kin, cousins, neighbors, spouses, and friends come to swim. It's a welcome break from the hot city pavements of Waterbury that grown-ups say "could fry an egg," not that anyone is known to have actually tried it.

Donal Keane and his brothers, Dan and Joe, his sister Dolly too, all work in the big brick factory that never sleeps. The family is so well represented there that going to the Scovill employees' recreation area on a scorching Sunday afternoon seems to them to be more of a right than a treat.

Donal's wife prepares lemonade and goes along for the ride, to cool down beneath those towering pines. Older than he by thirteen years and grown stout, which in her eyes precludes a bathing suit, she fans herself with the Sunday newspaper and shields her milk-white skin from the summer sun.

The car they arrive in is black, with running boards. It's old for its time, and the idea that vintage will someday be considered a fashionable style is a notion that would make Donal laugh if you were to tell him so. The car's fawn-colored woolen upholstery is scratchy on bare arms and emits a musty, hot-cloth scent. Along the back of the car's long front seat is a velvet-covered cord for rear-seat passengers to pull against to extricate themselves when their destination is reached. Donal has hung a folded Beacon blanket there, in a faded American Indian style design. When Betty and Pat, his children, first asked where he'd gotten it, he'd replied, "I chased an Indian up a tree and took it from him." And as often as they ask him now about the blanket, they always get the same reply.

In their eyes, it's as likely an explanation as any. The woods of Wolcott surrounding the dam seem so strange and wild to their city eyes that a lurking Indian seems entirely possible. Even the names of the roads they take to get here, Woodtick and Wolf Hill, sound wild. And the construction of the dam itself along the narrow, shady roads around the reservoir is so subtly done by the Italians imported by the Scovill Company that it seems in places to have been here forever.

The lower dam, sometimes called the Cornelis Dam, is made of masonry and earth, with double spillways that look, to Betty, when the water is high, like waterfalls. The upper dam has cattails and lily pads, and sometimes a rowboat is seen idling along in its far reaches.

"Back in the day, ice used to be cut from the frozen water and stored in sawdust," Betty's Uncle Jimmy has told her. But right now, in the heat of summer, this seems impossible, a fable told to while away the Sunday afternoon. So, too, are stories of lost farms underneath the water, flooded to make the dam that feeds the Scovill Company's mills down in the heart of Waterbury.

"Pasture lands for the cows, roads, and even stone walls, all were lost under the water," Uncle Jimmy has said. Lost things appeal to Betty, who loves a mystery as much as she loves secrets. And in her eyes, this tale of the dam's creation provides both. The employees' swimming place is on the lower dam, where loads of pale sand have been trucked in to make a beach.

Up above this domesticated area, in the wild places, the Scovill Rod and Gun Club members go about their activities in the appropriate seasons. In this year of 1936, a fishing permit can be had for only fifty cents.

There's an area above the swimming place that Betty has heard about and craned her neck to see, looking up at the tall pines above the spillway that rushes coolly downward without ceasing. Sometimes a few men and the occasional brave boy go up there through the forest path to dive from a rock formation into a deep part of the dam. Legend has it that there is a ledge down under the water, a long, shallow outcropping where untold numbers of swimmers have lost rings and medals, pocket change and keys, and once, it is reported, a shoe. It's not possible to see the diving rock from where Betty stands, and she has never been above there herself. Her mother has forbidden it. So for Betty, it has become a mystery story that she tells herself on the nights that she can't sleep.

"Would you like to go there?" Betty asks her little brother.

"I would," Pat answers, "but I'd be afraid."

"Of Mam?" she exclaims, well aware that Pat, in their mother's eyes, can do no wrong.

"Of Indians," he replies with a mock shiver.

"We'll go when Mam is napping," Betty tells him. "We'll need to wear our shoes because of rocks," she continues, although to herself, she admits it is actually in case of snakes.

Looking back over their shoulders, they begin. Their bathing suits are navy woolen ones, produced for them by their friend Ted, a lady who lives on the third floor of their house. Ted has a friend with children just a bit older than they are, and the growth spurt of those anonymous children has produced a bathing suit bounty. The shoes Betty and Pat have on are brown leather with laces, damned in their eyes as nearly all the other children have summery white canvas ones with rubber soles, but Mam has explained that sneakers are out of the budget question this summer.

"We'll rise above it, Pat," Betty has told her brother.

The afternoon sun is warm on their backs; the narrow dirt path is quiet. They have the woods all to themselves. The sounds of children calling out to each other at the beach grow muffled as they climb higher, and by the time they reach the diving rock, Betty and Pat hear nothing but the sound of their own panting.

"We should have brought a drink," Pat says.

"There's a whole lake here," Betty tells him. "Have a drink of that."

"But I don't have a cup!"

"Just bend down and put your face in. You'll be okay."

Both of them notice at the same time that the dark water is opaque, probably because of its depth.

"Something could be down there," Pat whispers.

"Oh, Pat, the lost things are down there. That's the whole point of this," Betty tells him. "So put your arm in and feel around."

"Yours is longer," he replies.

And so they both kneel and reach in.

"How deep is this?" Pat asks. The ground where they are kneeling is worn free of grass. It's hard-packed dirt with a few pebbles that cause him to wince and shift his weight back a bit to relieve his bare knees.

"Oh, maybe a mile," Betty guesses. In school last year, her class studied the Grand Canyon, and a taste for big spaces has stayed with her.

"So how far down is the ledge?" he continues.

"Not so far. Jimmy Black dove down once and saw it. But he couldn't hold his breath long enough to get his hands on anything."

"But you could, Betty. You could dive down. You took swimming lessons from Ted. And she's the Red Cross lady!"

While they've been talking, Pat has removed his hand from the dark water. He's not so sure that the dam does not eat stuff or that ghosts from those lost farms he's heard about aren't on the lookout to capture boys for underwater work.

"I could go down," Betty muses. "I can hold my breath for a long time."

The water is shockingly cold as she eases in, feet first, unwilling to dive into the unknown. It's of a temperature that their father, the eternal optimist, would describe as bracing. Betty holds her nose closed with one hand and disappears from view.

It's too quiet for Pat's comfort up in the woods on his own. Pat is hoping that Betty will return with a fist full of dimes and quarters. And he hopes it won't take long. He begins to plan. First would come a pair of those white canvas summer shoes and money for a daily Hershey's bar. He'd like to go to the movies at the Alhambra every Saturday afternoon. And a black Raleigh bicycle would really be something to show his friends.

The water feels warmer once you're in it for a bit, Betty has found. Opening her eyes, she looks around. It's like a blurry silent movie under the water. Straight ahead is a wall of brown dirt with a few tree roots showing white. A school of minnows circles above where a shaft of sun hits the surface. Betty looks down but cannot see the ledge. Out of breath, she surfaces.

"No luck yet," she tells her brother. "I'll try again." This time she goes deeper, where the water is murky. She sees what might be a ledge, but it proves unreachable. As she pushes her way to the top, she sees something glimmering out of the corner of her eye. On her third try, she grabs it.

"What did you get?" Pat asks. Betty opens her hand. It's a Saint Christopher medal on a broken chain.

"It was caught on a root poking out of the bank. That ledge must be really deep. I can't find it."

The way back is quiet, the air heavy with disappointment.

"I wish I'd been able to get there," Betty says. "If I'd found money, I'd have given it to Mam to put aside." The unspoken end of this sentence is known to both children, as there have been weeks when their father's pay takes a detour to the tavern on its way back up the hill to Walnut Street.

Pat drags the toe of his shoe through the dirt, embarrassed for his dreams of what he'd have done with the money. Betty's thoughtfulness makes his ideas sound like something he'd need to tell Father Jim in confession.

"Oh, and Pat," Betty adds, putting her hand on his bony shoulder as if sensing his thoughts, "of course we'd have gotten something nice for you as well."

When they return, it's time to leave for home.

"Your mother was looking for you two. I told her you were helping me to put the water wings away," says the ever watchful Ted, signaling them to silence. Ted's brown bathing suit has a big white badge with a Red Cross in its center sewn onto it, as befits the Scovill swimming area's instructor. Thanks to her, their adventure has gone undetected.

"Dad? How far down is the ledge?" asks Betty from the deep backseat of their car.

"The whole dam is about thirty feet deep, so I'm told. You'd need five six-foot men standing on each other's shoulders to reach the bottom. In a word, that ledge is unlikely to be found."

Their failed quest has lost its luster. And a second trip up through the woods to the enigmatic reservoir which holds its secrets as tightly as Egypt's sphinx is one neither Betty nor Pat wishes to make. It seems more sensible to devote the rest of their summer to swimming. September sends them back to Saint Mary's School, and thoughts of the ledge take a backseat to homework. The trees are losing their leaves and sweaters are the order of the day when Donal comes home one night with news.

"They're draining the reservoir to fix a crack in the dam," he tells them. "The whole of it will be exposed."

"Would you be able to see the ledge, Dad?" they ask, nearly in unison.

"Sure, you'd see the whole of the reservoir, bottom, top, and sides."

"Can we go? Will you take us?"

Rolling a cigarette from his tobacco can and a pack of Zig-Zag papers to go with his after-supper cup of tea, Donal agrees.

"We'll take a ride on Sunday after Mass."

To Donal, it's a ride. To Betty and Pat, it's a mission. The thought of viewing the bottom of the mysterious reservoir and its famed ledge is so exciting that it makes even their preparations for Halloween and the anticipated collection of free candy and pennies at night while dressed as a witch and a ghost take a backseat. Hands down, the reservoir's draining is the event of the season.

"But how does the water get out?" asks Pat.

"The caretaker opens the floodgates on the dam, and out she goes," Donal replies.

"Goes where, Dad?"

"Goes down the Mad River, all the way to the Naugatuck River. And at long last, the river makes its way to the sea."

"Does it go to Ireland?" asks Betty.

"I suppose it might. Eventually. Stranger things have happened," Donal muses.

The children chew over that idea until their father draws up at the recreation area.

"Everyone out," he calls, holding open their car door with a flourish like a pretend chauffeur.

How bare the swimming area looks with its lifeguard chair and picnic benches put away for the winter. And how open the place looks with the leaves falling fast from the trees. They take the path up to the reservoir, noting that they can see behind them all the way to the road where they have left their car.

Standing at the spot where they stood on that day last summer, they look down into the reservoir and across to the far side. It's like a bowl with a mud bottom. Autumn leaves have drifted down in piles. They see a few lines of field stones that must have once been walls for the farms and are surprised to learn that the old houses were torn down before the land was flooded.

Directly below them is a shallow pool where Pat glimpses movement. Perhaps it is a fish. Out in the middle, about a dozen men are walking, hunting for whatever they can find.

"Look, Pat! It's the ledge." Betty points to a spot protruding from the steep wall. It looks to be about two feet deep and a yard long. Clearly it's too far down for them to have ever reached it. Discovering that this is so makes them feel better about their secret, unsuccessful trip.

"Nothing much to see here, I'd say," Dad comments. Betty and Pat are forced to agree.

"Out for a rubbernecking, are you?" Tom Cronin has arrived upon the scene, walking his little beagle, Toby.

"We wanted to see the ledge," Betty replies. "But there's nothing on it."

"Ah, the ledge was the first place searched on Monday when the water drained away."

"We heard it was full of treasure," Pat tells him.

"And so it was. Treasure of a sort. All depending, of course, on who you are."

Lighting his pipe with a match struck on the bark of a nearby tree, he continues.

"There were eyeglasses found, and keys, an undershirt, and close to three dollars worth of change. And in the middle of a pile of rusted bottle caps, sat Jack Reilly's Leavenworth high school ring, class of 1929. A treasure, for him, I'd say."

"Wait till I tell the boys at school about this," Pat exults. He tosses a stick for Toby that lands down in the mud far below. Toby barks, too wise to follow it.

"Frost tonight, I warrant," says Mr. Cronin, mostly to himself.

It occurs to Betty that they are standing in the middle of a story: the summer that has passed, the summer yet to come. When the water returns the reservoir will look the way it always has. But now she knows how the water goes out and gets in. And most important, she now knows the exact location of the legendary shelf. Her curiosity is satisfied.

Betty buttons her sweater and puts her hands deep into the pockets of her plaid skirt. In a week or two, the ledge will be back under its watery blanket, hidden beneath the ice and snow, waiting to fill again with next summer's lost treasures.

"I'm glad we came, Dad," she says.

"Knowledge is power, after all," he replies.

Betty feels more grown up, somehow, now that she's made this trip. But the late afternoon is turning cold, too cold to stand around and think deep thoughts about it.

"Race you," says Pat, tapping her on the shoulder as if they are playing tag. And he and Betty run ahead to where they've left the car.

SATURDAY NIGHT SWELLS

The single family house is white clapboard, crowned with a widow's peak gable above its green front door. The roofline in the front is amazingly uneven, swooping down with a quirky flourish on the left side of the door only, all the way to the ground. It sits on a wide double lot in Waterbury's north end, a lucky thing for the house since it has so many varied additions, front and back and sides.

Amber Court is the house's street address, and it's there, on Saturday nights, that a select group of couples go by invitation to dance. They enter in twos, these Scovill factory workers on their night out, the men in tuxedos or dark suits, their hands scrubbed clean with bars of Lava soap and a stiff brush, the women in full-skirted, pastel-colored dance dresses of chiffon or tulle, their hair permanent waved into ringlets or pinned up in the occasional French twist.

It's 1939, and the songs of the year are dreamy ones. Glen Miller's "Moonlight Serenade," Larry Clinton's "Deep Purple," waft on the air from radio station WATR. The dance is something to think about all week while you're kicking a press or pouring molten brass.

Betty is in high school, a sophomore at Leavenworth High. And she has dancing on her mind too. Last spring, she was invited to the junior prom by a dark-haired boy named Rob. But her father wouldn't hear of it.

"Let your Uncle Dan take you," he'd suggested. "He has a dark suit." Dad is clueless about high school dances, and Betty can't blame him for not understanding since he never went to one. She'd stayed home and sat at the bedroom window, looking out into the night sky, wishing on stars, and well aware of being overly dramatic.

It's summer now, and this year, the place the family is calling home is a rent at the top of North Main Street near City Mills. There is a long, grassy side yard with a rustic gazebo in its center fashioned from saplings. Under its shingled roof are bench seats, and along the sides of the gazebo up against the foundation, mint grows wild, releasing its cool scent when it is stepped on.

Their landlady, Mrs. Mazzacotta, is always hungry for a chat. She often invites Betty and her mother to join her on summer afternoons. They sit and listen to Mrs. Mazzacotta's radio in the background. It's on a shelf inside her kitchen, its volume turned up high. The music blends with the drone of traffic and the twitter of the birds that flock down from Lakewood Park to roost in the trees around them.

This particular house is on the fringes of the densely populated middle of North Main Street and borders the more rural section of the miles long road that slopes upward to intersect Lakewood Road.

"Caught in the middle" is how Mrs. Mazzacotta describes her house.

"Too much noise now" is how she begins her daily saga of how the world is going to the dogs.

"All the wrong kind of people," she continues. Betty's mother nods. It's not her issue. She is simply being gracious to her hostess.

"They come to our city to work in the factories," says the landlady. "Immigrants. People from down South. What are you going to do?" she concludes, throwing her hands up, seemingly forgetting that she was once an immigrant herself.

For a while they sit in silence, listening to the radio. But after a while, the music becomes another helping of food for Mrs. Mazzacotta's thought.

"And another thing," she says, "some of this music I don't like. Now Kate Smith," she continues, as the radio program concludes with "God Bless America," "now there's a woman for you. And that's what I call a song."

Even though it is a big city, Waterbury is a small town at heart. And news spreads fast, especially news that some folks might call gossip.

"Have you heard about the Saturday night dances?" people ask each other.

It is Damson Pierrot who has begun them. He and his wife Evangeline have even added a ballroom on to the side of their house. It's said that the room is thirty feet long, with a hardwood floor that shines like glass, inviting jokes about being able to see the ladies' underwear reflected in a certain light.

Because so many people in Betty's family work at Scovill's, they have firsthand knowledge of the couple in question.

"They're louche," says Aunt Dolly. Newly wed to her policeman beau, she has donned an evening gown herself lately for the policemen's ball at the Armory, waltzing decorously on the arm of her uniformed partner. But in her eyes, this is not the same.

"It is a different situation entirely with us. Like comparing chalk to cheese," she tells them. Dolly works with Evangeline in the assembly line doing bench work and does not believe she is really French.

"It's *merci* this and *merci* that," Dolly sniffs.

Evangeline is Dolly's supervisor. And even in a head scarf and coveralls, it's clear from her bright red lipstick and matching lacquered nails that Evangeline has pizzazz. If Betty's father had been at home when his sister Dolly held forth, he'd have made his voice go squeaky and called out, "Meow!" But he is at work, and so Dolly's opinion stands unchallenged.

Damson Pierrot is a foreman in the casting department. Neither he nor his wife is over five feet tall. But for a small man, he has an unexpectedly deep voice. He also has what Betty's aunt calls bedroom eyes. Damson is good at his job, and the men respect him. He glides effortlessly around the shop on his small feet that seem made for dancing pumps. The men wouldn't dare to ask questions about his life.

The women, however, feel no such need for reserve.

"Tell about your dance dresses," they coax Evangeline. And she is only too happy to oblige.

"The new one I'll wear this Saturday is yellow," she begins, "with a little silk stole and a big silk sash. I put my winter ones away in the cedar closet. I hated to pack away the red velvet winter one with the white fur collar. That one is my favorite."

It's said that Damson makes his wife's gowns himself. Her sister Esmeralda also works at Scovill's, and has confirmed this tantalizing piece of information over a cigarette at break time. And Esmeralda ought to know because she lives in the house on Amber Court too. Some folks at work have suggested that theirs is a ménage à trois. But that is merely conjecture. It's something that no one really knows for sure.

Across the street from Betty, on the second floor of a triple-decker house, live Bertha and Stanley Dolinsky. Betty knows the young couple from swimming at Scovill's Dam. She knows they go to the dances, and so she asks Bertha about them.

"You want the lowdown, I guess," Bertha laughs. "Well, it's like this. You have to be married to go. There is no hanky-panky allowed. We all eat supper before we dance, in a knotty pine room with card tables laid end to end and folding chairs. The women bring covered dishes for potluck. There's whiskey if you want a highball, and at the end of the night, we have cake and coffee."

"Is there really a ballroom?" asks Betty.

"You bet! And a big record player with so many records I wouldn't be able to count them. There's a big speaker to make the music loud, and every week, Damson and Evangeline do a demonstration dance of a new step for us to practice. Her shoes are silver, with a little strap across the instep so they won't come off even when he dips her at the end."

Bertha pauses for a moment in her kitchen, wiping her hands on a dish towel.

"You should see it," she continues. "Real palm trees in pots, all of us in fancy clothes. It's beautiful, Betty. It's like a dream."

Betty has been thinking the same thing herself, that she should see it. That night, she asks her brother if he'll go with her on Saturday night to have a look. Pat agrees. At thirteen, he is ripe for adventure. Their mother waves good-bye from the gazebo. They've had an early supper of cold ham and salad because of the July heat. The dancing doesn't begin till seven, so they have plenty of time to get there.

On Amber Court, the preparations for the evening are nearly finished. Damson has selected the records for tonight's music and stacked them in order next to the record player. Esmeralda and Evangeline have spread the tablecloths and set out the dishes.

"Do we have ice?" Esmeralda asks her sister.

"Ha, ha," says Damson, coming around the corner. "You want ice? Is it too hot for you girls? I can make it even hotter," he continues, twirling an imaginary moustache. He chases them around the tables. They retreat, giggling, to their bedrooms that are lined up next to each other on the far side of the ballroom floor.

"Just call if you need my help getting dressed," he says.

Betty and Pat have gotten all the way down North Main Street, nearly into the center of this part of town that is known locally as the Square. As they pass the Alhambra Theater, they pause to examine the poster inside the little glass door with the heading Current Attraction.

A dramatic Bette Davis with downcast eyes is in a halo of light. *Dark Victory* is tonight's offering.

"I'd rather see *Stagecoach*," Pat says. "I like the cowboys."

They begin to zigzag through the uphill streets and cross streets: Easton, Hazel, Crown. At Hopkins, they slow down. Amber Court is just around the corner, and Betty doesn't want to be seen.

"We're like a couple of stage-door Johnnies," Pat laughs, "the kind Aunt Dolly is always claiming are up to no good."

Betty likes the house's tidy white picket fence. Pat jokes about its three brick chimneys, speculating on which one Santa climbs down to bring his Christmas gifts. They've arrived at Amber Court just in time for the show they've come to see.

The guests arrive promptly. Some drive cars, and a few have walked from nearby homes. The ladies look like they are going to a prom, Betty thinks. The men follow along, carrying the covered casseroles.

The front door opens, and a small man in a white dinner jacket greets his guests by name and ushers them inside.

"Look, Betty. There's Bertha Dolinsky," says Pat, pointing to their blond neighbor in her lavender dress. You'd never guess that just a few hours ago Bertha was in pin curls in her backyard, hanging out the laundry.

If these folks are, as their Aunt Dolly has labeled them, "Saturday night swells," Betty cannot see what is wrong with that.

"I wish I could go inside too," she tells Pat. "All dolled up to dance. I wish I could go there with Rob."

Pat eyes his sister but says nothing. A year ago he'd have hooted at her confession. But now, at thirteen, he has begun to see the whole boy-girl thing from a different perspective. Once the couples have all arrived, the door of the house swings closed.

"It's going to take a while for them to eat supper," Pat says. "Let's go back to Rinaldi's corner store. They have Dixie Cup ice creams in their freezer."

By the time they return, they can hear music. The song is "Tea for Two."

"Oh boy. A cha cha," calls Pat, doing a little kick step in the street.

"I've got to have a look," Betty tells him. Curiosity overrides her fear of being accused of trespass. And so Betty crosses the side lawn to the large curtained window. It takes up nearly the whole side of the house. She feels certain that this must be the location of the fabled ballroom.

Even though the heavy drapes are lined and drawn, there is a place at one end where she can see in if she turns sideways and closes one eye. Betty can see one of the palm trees Bertha told her about.

"Let's go now," Pat says. "I'm bored."

"Wait," Betty tells him. "I'm not through."

The music has started up again. This time the song is "Stairway to the Stars." The dancers take to the floor, the couples holding each other close. These dancers know all the steps. Some of them are even dancing with their eyes closed. It's as if they are in another world.

The scene fills Betty with longing. For what, she can't exactly put into words. It's a feeling without a name, but it's a deep one. How quiet it is outside on the narrow street. Betty turns her face from the window and feels a tiny breeze that smoothes her hair like a gentle hand.

"Okay," she tells Pat. "We can go now. I've seen enough."

What she has suddenly understood is that Damson Pierrot has created more than just a night out in Brass City, more than a chance for his coworkers to get all dressed up. Whether or not he intended them to be so, his dances are a gift to the dancers. And his little white house in the heart of the North End has become, at least on Saturday nights, a portal to a better world.

This notion of Betty's is perhaps just wishful thinking. But still, knowing that ordinary people can have extraordinary moments is a wonderful discovery. She hums the last dance tune as they walk home.

In The Garden

Ordinary days are best, he thinks, the days when nothing happens that will cause you to play the story over in your mind, inventing outcomes that might have proved more serendipitous. If Donal was a student of philosophy, he'd no doubt agree with Henry David Thoreau, who'd warned folks, "Beware of all enterprises that require new clothes."

But Donal reads only the morning *Waterbury Republican* and its evening companion, the *American,* and an occasional back copy of the *Kerryman* that comes to their house courtesy of his sister-in-law in Killarney.

Over there, in Ireland, Donal worked as a gardener. In the years since he's lived in America, he's come full circle. Beginning at Scovill's Brass, he's gone from that job to the Waterbury clock shop, and now at last, and far best to his mind, the Park Department of the city he calls home. Hamilton Park where he has risen to the rank of foreman has a rose garden on its Silver Street side that is a showplace. Postcards of it are sold in local stores.

The many varieties and colors of the exquisite flowers are at their peak in June. But the thing about the roses that Donal loves best is that they get their second wind and put on another show in early September. For something so seemingly delicate, roses are quite plucky, he thinks. And he is plucky too. As a lad, Donal's mother often told him that his name meant "ruler of the world." He thinks that he may have taken this information a bit too much to heart, at least when it came to choosing a wife. What he'd imagined when he'd set his sights on the daughter of Mr. Finn was that he'd be taken into the family. In time, he'd imagined, he'd be one of them, with the run of the place.

His was a plan that included such details as a handsome new dark suit of clothes and perhaps one day, a motor car. For sure there'd be a silver christening mug for the baby that was on the way. But never could he have foreseen being hounded from Killarney by the old man he'd thought to call father after he'd married nor himself a family man at seventeen with not a penny to bless himself.

Well, it was all long ago. And the baby, his daughter Betty, is a grown woman with a daughter of her own. Donal is standing in the rose garden at that golden evening hour he likes best, just as the sun highlights the brass factory's brick walls. Beyond them, to the west, he can see the top of the train station's bell tower, a skyscraper of a monument with clocks on all four sides.

He takes a smoke from the breast pocket of his work shirt and leans against the white latticed gazebo. Here the roses are of a variety called Glad Tidings. The cigarettes are his own, rolled at the kitchen table from a tin of Old Bugler tobacco. The limpness of the cigarette paper belies their strength. It's the hour to be heading home, but Donal thinks there will be just enough time to stop at the Park Café for a shot. Whiskey neat is his drink, and one sometimes has a way of leading to another.

It's late when Donal fits his key into the lock of his house. The Forestville clock on the shelf above the kitchen sink chimes twelve. Upstairs in his bedroom, he lights a votive candle and prepares for bed. Above it hangs a lithograph printed on tin of Saint Therese of Lisieux, holding a bouquet of roses. The picture of this saint, also known as the Little Flower, measures nearly three feet square in its black wooden frame. Donal has never made the connection between her and his work in the rose garden, nor has he any recollection of how she came to hang on his wall in the first place. But the picture has been in the house for so long that Saint Therese has come to seem like friend, her brown eyes following his preparations with a gentle, familiar look of reproach.

The candle he has lit sits on the bureau top opposite his bed. Its glow is reflected in the attached looking glass. The top of the bureau is crowded with plaster saints, set in orderly rows around a central grouping of the Holy Family. No one, not even his wife or daughter, ever asks Donal what it is that he prays for: if it's something specific or merely a chronic piety.

He rolls on to his side, turns away from his thoughts, and falls asleep. The open window lets in a breeze that lifts the curtain, fans his face. Donal dreams of the lake in front of Dinis, his wife's girlhood home. In his dream, the lake is impossibly wide, its shore receding no matter how hard he rows his boat to cross it.

"Breakfast," Zora calls through the bathroom door where Donal is shaving with a cautious hand. It is their custom not to address each other by their Christian names. And when one speaks of the other to a third party, it is as "himself" and "herself." The formality of this has come to suit them. It's a way of keeping a polite distance.

"We've a letter from Ireland," Zora tells him, pointing to the pale blue envelope marked "par avion" set next to the sugar bowl.

Donal's soft-boiled egg sits before him in an egg cup shaped like a chicken with a basket on its back.

"It is from my sister Una," she adds.

"And what news?" he asks as he cracks the shell with the side of his spoon, adds salt, and digs in. It was Una that Donal fancied first, but she'd laughed when he'd declared his intentions.

"She has married," Zora replies, smoothing the veil on her hat. It's a blue one with a tiny spray of forget-me-nots on its side. Zora wears it in the house to cover her hair. Straight and fine, it never pleases her.

"And who is the lucky man?" Donal asks in a tone he imagines as casual.

"Pat Nolan it is. And Una had to take him into town to buy a wedding suit. He'd none of his own to wear to the church."

"'Tis love in bloom, so. We'll be sending them a christening mug next." Donal cannot resist the dig. Una, at fifty-six, is well past the childbearing years. He himself is forty. Zora cannot let this remark of his pass.

"I, at least, wish my sister luck. There was never a chance for Una to have her own life while our father was alive. He held us so close to home." Zora says nothing about their own union. And it is for sure that she makes no mention of her own age, which is fifty-three.

Their own marriage is so far in the past that Donal truly does not begrudge Pat Nolan's success in an area where he himself has struck out. When he has left for the day for work, Zora goes upstairs to change his bed. That and dust mopping are the only things she does in Donal's room. The condition of his bureau top and its shrine are left to him. In her own room, with its view of the long walkway that leads to their front door, she pauses, remembering last night and other late nights as well when she's looked down on him and watched him coming home.

Those are the times when she lies quiet in her bed till she hears him come up the stairs to his own room and settle in.

Waterbury, Connecticut, is half a world away from Killarney. Over there right now, it's afternoon. She considers Una's choice of Pat Nolan, a rough man with no prospects of his own. For sure, at her age, the choices are few. At least with their father dead, she can please herself, Zora thinks. And though she has always taken pleasure in telling her daughter about the high points of her girlhood in Ireland, tales of lost glories that drive Betty mad with longing for a way of life that could never possibly be hers, it is Zora's secret that she much prefers life here.

Below the house on Hamilton Avenue, she can see the CR&L bus go by with clockwork regularity. The bus is one of her great pleasures. It offers a convenient, dependable lift to the city's center where she can take a cup of tea at the Waldorf Cafeteria, walk through the stores, and perhaps bring home a bakery cake for something sweet for tea. There is central heat from the coal furnace and a telephone in her parlor, indoor plumbing and hot water from the taps for washing clothes in a machine. The ease of American life never ceases to delight her. If asked, "Are you happy?" she'd be hesitant to reply in the affirmative. Happiness is such a fleeting sensation. But as to the daily business of living? Zora finds it very good indeed.

Smartly dressed in her dark blue street dress and black pumps, Zora waits with her transfer ticket for the bus that will take her up Willow Street to her daughter's house. Behind her is Woolworth's where she has purchased a dollhouse-sized red and yellow plastic sewing machine with a tiny wheel that actually spins. The toy is a surprise for her granddaughter. On a hook on the pantry door at her daughter's house hangs a cotton housedress. There's also a pair of maroon felt slippers with a little pompom on each toe, which she has slit discreetly at the sides with a razor blade to accommodate her bunions. No doubt there will be a basket of clean laundry which she will offer to press. Zora likes the serenity of ironing and the process where all of the wrinkles disappear.

The sunny morning is still a bit cool, reminding her of the long summer days spent in Ireland, the endless, repetitive work of her family's tearoom, and the longer, empty nights. It was on just such a morning that she'd stood in the window of the big room overlooking the Middle Lake, spreading the crisply starched white linen cloths over the tables where the tourists would soon be seated. She'd looked up from her work and seen an auburn-haired man with a little dog coming up the path. Not a man, on closer observation. No, more a lad about the age of her brother Tom. It was something different to see, something to think about beyond the daily sameness of her thirty years on earth, and more of it ahead, endlessly, in a way that could make her grind her teeth if she dwelled on it. Heretic that she is, Zora wants more from life than what it has produced thus far.

But she and Una are so carefully shepherded, tucked away in the white house on its tiny island between lakes. And each night at dusk, their father locks the gates across the two bridges. He says it is to keep strangers out. But Zora thinks that it is also to keep them all within. What "more" might be and how one might get it are questions she thinks about while she sits in the parlor each night, watching the fire as her parents go over the day's receipts.

Soon enough, though, she will learn that the name of the young man she glimpsed is Donal. He will know hers as well, as they take their first steps toward each other. The day has been a turning point for them, the scales of their separate pasts unbalanced by the introduction of something new. And it will change them both in ways they could never have foreseen.

On board her bus, Zora settles into a double seat behind the driver, her handbag next to her to preclude another passenger from joining her. When he has finished work, Donal will call for her at Betty's house. They'll have supper, sit on the front porch for a bit in the striped canvas deck chairs, then drive home. Despite his occasional detours on the way home from work, she feels she has made a good bargain, since it has carried her here to America. Zora arranges her skirts around her knees for modesty, rests one white gloved hand on her purse. It is a pleasant day, indeed, she thinks. Alone in her seat, she smiles.

At Hamilton Park, the roses are in full bloom. Donal surveys his kingdom. The bushes are watered and the blossoms deadheaded. The grassy walks are mowed. It's quitting time, and he drives to his daughter's house with the car windows rolled down, taking in the sweetness of the June air. He's remembering a day when he was seventeen. He'd worn his new white shirt that morning, carefully saved for an important occasion. He and his little Jack Russell terrier, Dandy, a crack at hunting rabbits, had set out for Dinis. He'd taken his bicycle, the dog running alongside. He'd thought to ask Mr. Finn for work. He knew he had the knack for making things grow, and old Finn's property was a large one. In his opinion, it seemed a likely match.

In the front window of the house, he'd glimpsed a woman staring out. A bit old for him, of course, but she'd caught his eye and held his glance. It was as if they'd met before. *I grinned and gave a nod,* he remembers. *The ease of it, standing at Finn's door poised to knock. A morning of possibilities, it was. Yet never did I foresee the one in store for me.* Donal slows the car, extends his left arm to signal the come around motion that means a right hand turn, and pulls into Betty's drive.

By ten o'clock that night, Zora has retired upstairs and closed her bedroom door. Donal lingers in the kitchen to wind the clock. Beneath the sink in a cabinet is a red glass decanter with a matching stopper. On its side, in bas relief, is a clipper ship in full sail. Why not? he thinks, remembering how his father had often observed that "a drink's good company." He pours himself a shot and turns out the light.

In his bedroom, he undresses and lights his evening candle with an Ohio Blue Tip from the match safe on the wall. The candle flickers shadows on the bed and walls, his freckled hands, and face. Donal recalls a pledge taken long ago in church to abstain from alcoholic drink and his membership back in Ireland in an organization called the Pioneers that advocated teetotalism. The candle was for that, at first, a prayer to stay dry. But now, the end lost sight of, it's become simply a habit with the comfort of an old routine. The light is a friendly presence in his room at the end of each day. It is company in the darkness and a wish for his good night.

RIVERSIDE

Cora has always awakened early, even as a girl back in Massachusetts. Then it was because of the horses neighing in her father's livery stable. Now it's the sound of the Worden's Dairy truck braking on Summit Street as the milkman makes his 5:00 am delivery. From the front windows of her parlor, she can look across Riverside Street to the big gray three-family house where she lived back when she first came to Waterbury.

Hers was the top-floor rent, tucked under the eaves of the slate roof. Cora delighted in its slanting ceilings as a cozy nest for her family of three children. The charm of the built-in cupboards and the spacious pantry almost made up for her husband's family, who considered her an unsuitable wife and took every opportunity to make their feelings known.

"Well, I did steal him from another woman," she tells herself, remembering her days working at Hemingway's mill in Watertown with Mike's old girlfriend when she was fifteen. She remembers her sixteen-year-old self as a mother, Mike away in France as a doughboy in the Great War. Cora needed to keep on working, and so she arranged with her landlady to watch her baby. From her machine on the top floor of the thread mill, Cora could just glimpse his wicker carriage in the backyard of the rooming house if he'd been put outside on a good day for fresh air. But at times when the carriage shook and she knew that her baby was crying, it was hard not to be able to go and comfort him.

I did the best I could, she thinks. *And when the Red Cross lady came and tried to take him away from me because I was too young, I wouldn't let her.* That baby, Mike Junior, is grown up and a father himself. But it is Cora's last baby, Rob, whom she favors most of her three children, and the idea of seeing him every day if they lived together has given her an idea.

Cora has had houses on her mind lately. Although she has never owned a house before, she's begun to think it's time. Rob and his wife are talking about buying one so that their daughter Betts can have a backyard to play in. So far, they haven't found one they can swing on Rob's pay at the telephone company, the place he calls Ma Bell. Cora hasn't said anything yet, but she has been figuring. She's decided that if she and Mike go in on the house purchase, then together they can make it happen.

From her current address on the west side of the Naugatuck River, Cora has a panoramic view of the gold dome of City Hall, the twin spires of Saint Anne's Church, and Pine Hill beyond them in the east. Her husband's family has lived in this end of town, the south end known locally as Brooklyn, since they arrived from Canada back in the last century.

"Back in the high button shoe era," she sniffs, knowing Mike's relatives won't like the idea of them moving away. They'll say Cora is trying to rise above her station. But the idea of their disapproval is like catnip to her. It sets her to tying on her apron and making Mike's favorite poached eggs on buttered toast for breakfast. She plans to prime him this morning for a conversation that will change their lives.

"Grandma Cora!" shouts Betts as she comes in the kitchen door ahead of her parents. "Grandma! Let's play outside." Outside is an ongoing problem if it means the deep, grassy backyard with its huge white hydrangea bushes and the landlady's tabby cat. The landlady, whom Cora considers a crabby old maid, has put her yard off-limits.

Cora thinks there must be a landlady school somewhere that coaches them on how to give tenants a bad time. To make the best of things, she's hung a swing in the long, narrow back hall, and it's there that she pushes Betts back and forth through the pale sunshine that arrows in through the glass on the back door in late afternoon.

There is no park in Brooklyn. Folks here often substitute a walk in the Riverside Cemetery, a green oasis in this part of town. Cora takes Betts there as a matter of course when she visits. They enter the black iron gates, pass the stone chapel with its pointy spire, and walk up the winding paths. Once inside, they are surrounded by monumental statues commemorating the haughty dead who were once the city's kingpins.

"Did we bring bread to feed the swans?" Betts always asks. Even though she is afraid of the big birds, she still likes to see them arch their long necks as they glide up to the edge of the lower pond. Once, the black swan chased an old man in a dark suit and fedora hat. You'd think it would have been a funny sight, but neither of them felt like laughing from the safety of their vantage point, a secluded bench of iron filigree on the hill above. If Cora had voiced her feelings, it would have been to say that they were interlopers themselves at Riverside, and their presence merely tolerated.

Some of the dead, perhaps the most elite of them, are asleep in little granite houses with their family names carved above the iron doors. One house has a weeping life-sized bronze woman pressing against its front door as if she could change the course of events. "Yet shall he live," insists the inscription on the tomb.

"Good luck," Cora tells the statue. Up toward the Draher Street stone wall, at the top of the hill, is the unexpected statue of a full-sized elk standing sentinel. He seems at home in the park in a way they will never feel. Sometimes they bring cookies and a little thermos of milk along, to picnic on their favorite bench. If it's strange to use the cemetery as a park, well, too bad, Cora tells the statue of a Civil War hero. The delicious scent of baking bread permeates the day. Brooklyn Bakery, around the corner on John Street, is at work creating its daily loaves of bread, both pumpernickel and rye.

"Let's go, now. We'll stop and pick up some doughnuts for Grandpa's tea," Cora tells Betts, who needs no coaxing when a visit to the bakery is in the offing.

Brooklyn is its own little town within the big city. You would never have to leave it unless you chose to. It has a movie theater, a shoe repair, a market, clothing stores, two Catholic churches, even a funeral parlor. But the more Cora thinks about it, the more she sets her heart on moving across the Naugatuck River to a fresh start.

It's Betty who begins the hunt for a house. She takes Betts with her one day by bus to the Green where they walk up into the Hillside neighborhood. They see a little house on Linden Street that would be perfect for the three of them. But the deal is to find a place for five, so they move on. The next one, a Victorian monstrosity on Central Avenue, is too big. That weekend they all ride in Mike's car to Willow Street to see a house with possibilities. It's not the "just right" fit that

Goldilocks found at the three bears' residence, but it has a front and back staircase, four rooms on each floor, and a big backyard.

Cora and Mike like the big windows on the second floor that will be theirs. Rob is pleased with the basement's workbench. And Betts likes the big backyard. Only Betty is silent. She does not want to live with her mother-in-law. But when the papers are signed, clinching the deal, the deed of ownership reads: Binette and Binette.

The curtains have been hung, and Cora has unpacked her dishes. There's a brand-new Castro convertible in her parlor and mahogany twin beds in the bedroom. New furniture was part of the attraction of moving, and Cora takes a homemaker's pride in the pineapple carved finials of her beds and the multicolored flowers on her couch.

But the bathroom with the tub is upstairs at Cora's and the clothesline access is downstairs at Betty's. And there is only one telephone between them. The temptation to listen in on the extension when it rings is sometimes too great for them to overcome.

Rob and Mike hear all about it over supper each night, and by consensus, they begin on outdoor projects that will take them out of hearing range of conflicts.

"It's like two dogs barking at each other," Rob says.

"More like two cats meowing," Mike replies. "But they'll get over it. They'll have to."

On Sunday afternoons, Mike and Cora go for a drive. It's Betty's opportunity to go upstairs and have a look around. There's nothing to find, of course, it's just an assertion of her rights, a territorial thing.

On the rare occasions when Betty goes out and Cora babysits, she, too, looks. But Cora is not as careful to hide her traces as Betty is. One day, Betty retaliates with a note tucked into her nightgown drawer, a note that reads, "Hello, Mom! Did you find what you were looking for?" That night there is no communication from the second floor of their house and a silence that can only mean that the arrow has found its mark.

It's a silence that could be interpreted as peace, so they go with it. Betty stays in her own kitchen when Cora's family visits. They come in little groups of two or three, to have cake and coffee and regale each other with what Betty calls their "goings on." For such runty little people, they really are lively, Betty thinks. One nephew plays the accordion and one is a country-and-western singer. A brother breeds chinchillas in his basement; a sister has an ex-husband with a genuine ballroom in his house.

Betty's own family are serious folks, she feels. The ladies, in particular, are placid, pigeon-bosomed women with sensible lace-up shoes, given to white gloves and daily rosaries. She keeps Betts downstairs when Cora's family visits, fearing contamination from unorthodox ideas. But it's too late. At five, going on six, Betts is all ears. She sits on the front stairs to listen to the accordion music and to hear about the alligators and orange groves the Florida brother has seen. It's better than a bedtime story.

And then there are Cora's girl friends from her thread mill days. One has brightly rouged cheeks and red lipstick. The other, less colorful, speaks only French.

"We need a doorman around here," Betty tells Rob after her sister-in-law, whom she dismisses as flashy, arrives to give Cora a permanent wave. It's not in Betty's nature lately to be gregarious. She finds herself becoming obsessed with keeping things in perfect order, and guests do not fit with her new agenda.

Cora's friends ask her if she misses Brooklyn and its conveniences. She does not. The bus stops on the opposite side of the street to her new house, and downtown's shops are classier and much more numerous. It's a delight to dress up and go downtown, to walk in and out of the shops to see what's new. Cora does not consider herself a clothes horse, no matter what her sisters-in-law say. She simply likes nice things and takes note of how they are made. It's a habit learned from her French mother, who sewed for a living. Cora sews too. Betts's white voile christening dress, tucked away now in her cedar chest in blue tissue paper, has a smocked bodice, its bonnet and coat embroidered with French knots and tiny fleur de lis.

Back on Riverside Street, Cora used to walk to the Saint Anne's convent once a week to learn fine embroidery and cutwork from the nuns. She'd take a kitchen chair out onto the back porch up there on the third floor after her household chores were done and enjoy the breeze and the view of the city as she worked. Happily, there aren't as many chores to do in her new digs, and the front porch on Willow is reserved for summer evenings rather than afternoons, since it faces west, so Cora has set to work on some summer dresses and matching aprons for herself. Cora notices, when she glances down the front stairs of their shared hall, that Betty has begun to wash the porch down with soap and water every morning in a way that seems excessive. She mentions it to Mike that night and adds that she is going to offer to watch Betts so Betty can work part-time.

Rob isn't pleased, but as luck would have it, there's an opportunity at the nurses' registry for private duty work on the Hillside. Betty whitens her shoes, starches her uniform, and begins.

"It's fun up here in your house, Grandma," Betts confides from her perch, standing on the back of Cora's couch. She is wearing one of Cora's sheer curtains as a makeshift bride's veil and lipstick that she has applied herself with a not too steady hand. As she balances, she waves the Hershey's bar she is eating in lieu of lunch. Cora is standing in the middle of the parlor, being fitted for a custom made contraption that in another era would have been called stays. Madame Rochet, known to her customers as the corset lady, has appeared on foot from her Waterville Street rooming house to make the final adjustments on Cora's undergarment, its flat metal bones concealed beneath a fabric of peach colored brocade.

"But Grandma lets me" has become a refrain downstairs in the house when Betty asserts her authority.

"I knew your mother would try to make trouble," Betty tells her husband.

"So stay home then," Rob replies, taking advantage of the situation to drive home his preference about work.

But Betty likes to work. And so she says no more until next morning on her way out the door when she pauses to let Cora know who is boss.

"When the cat's away, the mice will play," Cora says to Betts. "Don't tell your mother so much, and we'll be fine."

Christmas brings the bonanza of two trees under one roof and a television set for Cora and Mike. It's the first TV ever in the immediate family, and as amazingly as the magic act of Blackstone the Magician who played at the Palace Theater in 1922, the thirteen-inch screen black-and-white Motorola in its mahogany case unites them. Each evening that all four grown-ups settle in upstairs with the adventures of *Amos 'n Andy* or *I Love Lucy* enhances a truce between Betty and Cora that eventually ripens into détente. And Betts, whom they imagine tucked in bed asleep, sometimes climbs the stairs and sits on the floor behind them, peering around the corner of the living room's doorway from the drafty upstairs hall.

Although Betty has joined Saint Margaret's Church on Willow, Cora and Mike still drive to Brooklyn on Sundays for Mass at Saint Patrick's. Afterward, they go to Billy's for newspapers, Brooklyn Bakery for pastry, and perhaps to visit Mike's family on Riverside Street. Sometimes Betts goes along, too. She is fascinated by the stained-glass windows in the big gray stone church that tell the story of the life of Saint Patrick in glowing colors. Her favorite window shows the saint in a bright green cape driving purple snakes out of a Gorgon's head in Ireland, a feat the man is said to have accomplished once and for all, for eternity.

Equally fascinating to her is the river at the back of the family's Brooklyn property, at the end of the lot behind a row of gray garages. It's a given on every visit there that she'll be taken there by Mike to toss a few pebbles into the swiftly moving water. Betts can't say exactly why she loves the Naugatuck River, except that it seems alive as it hurries down the valley, oblivious to her and her carefully thrown stones.

Inside the big gray house, there are Toll House cookies and ginger ale on the first floor and intriguing corners to explore on the third. The second floor is where Mike's sister Maida lives. She is the matriarch of the family, as well as the current owner of the family homestead. It's always a formal, slightly edgy visit for them in her parlor, where the sun peers weakly through the stiffly starched lace curtains and her Royal Doulton figurines of elegant ladies watch from their perch on her mahogany whatnot shelf, their long china skirts held in their china hands as if they worry that something may dirty them.

"How are you faring in your new home?" is the usual question. Maida always seems crestfallen when they reply "Fine, thanks."

"The Binettes have been here since 1880," she reminds them. "And you will always be able to return to Brooklyn and to this house our father built."

"We're all right where we are," Mike tells his sister. "But thanks for the invite. It's good to know."

It's a mild, bright Easter Sunday, and Cora is wearing her new navy blue suit. Betts has a straw hat with a broad rim and a black velvet ribbon bow with long tails called streamers down its back. They are both wearing white gloves and carrying pocket books with rosaries in them, though in Betts case it is more to keep her occupied in church than because she is holy.

How solidly the three-family house stands on its granite-block foundation. Beneath its gabled slate roof, you can't even hear the traffic driving past along Riverside Street. If you told this family that in just a few more years the Naugatuck River will rise and sweep it all away, the house, two family members, and the Brooklyn neighborhood itself, they would laugh out loud. They would tell you that you were dreaming.

THE RICH ARE DIFFERENT

In her starched white cotton nurse's uniform, Betty feels transformed. White stockings, her crisp white cap with one thin line of black on its band, and she is good to go. She fastens the gray leather strap of her nurse's watch with its sweeping red second hand for taking a patient's pulse. Her rubber-soled oxfords, freshly whitened with Kiwi liquid polish last night, on top of the spread-out Sports section of the Waterbury *Republican-American*, are soundless on her kitchen's rose-colored linoleum floor.

You might think that an eight-hour private duty shift of cleaning up a cranky, bedridden old lady and listening to her complain wouldn't be the greatest of jobs to have. But in the evening or the late afternoon, depending on which shift she has drawn, and after Mrs. Goodly's shot of morphine knocks her out (Mrs. Goodly is an addict), Betty can sit back in an armchair in the Goodly drawing room and take her meal on a tray.

Prepared by Cook and brought to her by Euphonia, Mrs. Goodly's maid, it is served on the family china, specially commissioned in England for Elvira Goodly as a bride. There is an engraved picture of Mrs. Goodly's house in the center of each white plate, printed in brown and garlanded along the edge with tightly budded brown chrysanthemums. The house where Betty works is called Chrysanthemum Lodge. It's a Victorian extravaganza that is clearly on a downward spiral.

"Queen Anne," Mrs. Goodly calls it, reminding Betty of the lacy weeds that poke out of the cracks of the sidewalks on Walnut Street in the north end of town. That's where Betty grew up, in walking distance of Scovill's brass mill. The town is Waterbury. Betty has lived here all her life, so far. She is twenty-nine.

Betty and Euphonia are the same age. Although they live in the same city, they never would have met except for this job. Betty's house is around the corner from Mrs. Goodly's neighborhood. But most black families make their home in the city's North Square section. Integration has happened here in Waterbury as well as throughout the USA, although evidence of it is slower in the housing sector that some would like in this year of 1952. The women look forward to their chats. What they share of their daily routine warms them in the face of Elvira Goodly's frosty manner, which Betty refers to, though not to her employer's face, as her "Queen of the May" act.

It's nearly Easter, and the two young mothers have discussed Easter baskets and the best place to buy plush Easter bunnies for their daughters. Howland-Hughes on Bank Street has the best bunnies in delicate pastels. Their ears are lined in satin, and for only fifty cents extra, it is possible to have your child's name written in one ear in gold. Betty's daughter is seven. Her pink bunny that says "Elizabeth," Betts's actual baptismal name, is already purchased and tucked away upstairs on a shelf in Betty's mother-in-law's coat closet.

In the Goodly drawing room where Betty sits to dine, the fireplace is made of dark green marble, its tiny cupids holding garlands of roses picked out in tarnished gold. The heavy satin drapes are edged with a deep fringe that drags on the parquet floor. Perhaps they were green when they were new; an inner pleat where the sun has not discolored them seems to point to this. But time has turned them mostly pale gray. Betty had put her hand on one, when she first came to Chrysanthemum Lodge, to look out onto Hillside Avenue for a view of what the folks her mother has labeled the Other Half saw daily, and was nearly choked by the cloud of dust that escaped, unsettled by her touch.

"The rich really are different from us," she told her mother-in-law that night. "Yes, they buy the best of everything, but then that's the end of it. They never change a single thing again. Mrs. Goodly's stuff is falling apart." The women shake their heads together at this inexplicable behavior.

At Betty's house, her downstairs half of the small house shared with her husband's parents, the organdy tiebacks on the windows are washed and starched each month, then hung again with care to even spacing of their gathers. The linoleum kitchen floor is washed and waxed each Thursday night.

Mrs. Goodly's draperies and their condition puzzle Betty enough for her to ask about them.

"My drawing room was decorated in 1929, my dear, just before the 'crash.' It is top drawer," says her employer. "When one has purchased the best, one never feels the necessity to change. 'Do it once and do it right' is my motto."

A motto is something Betty has never thought about. What hers would be, if she had one, gives her something to think about on her walk home. The actual distance she covers from Chrysanthemum Lodge to Willow Street is a mere four blocks. But when you factor in lifestyle and time warp, the distance lengthens dramatically.

At home, Cora, Betty's mother-in-law, relinquishes charge of little Betty as soon as she returns. And Betty feels that when she takes off her uniform and becomes a housewife again, she completes a transformation that she privately likens to Cinderella.

"Well, that was another day in the bog," Betty tells Cora. It's an expression her parents brought with them from Killarney. It refers to a long day spent cutting turf to burn for the fire. Betty's work is not so hard at all, and she relishes her walks past the Hillside Avenue mansions. It is her time to dream.

"Mommy," little Betty calls. "Look at my wedding gown." She is wearing Cora's lace tablecloth, secured with a length of clothesline. It's an after school get-up appropriated for watching *The Big Payoff* quiz show on Cora's black-and-white TV. Men vie on this show for prizes for their girlfriends. The big payoff is a full length mink coat. At seven, there is no thought given to a groom. The gown's the thing. Prince Charming, to little Betty, is just a long-haired guy in tights from her storybook.

"I married my prince," Betty tells her daughter.

"Daddy," Betts agrees. Her dark-haired father is everyone's favorite.

Browning the pork chops for supper, Betty thinks back to their high school meeting, their secret romance and elopement in December of 1941, just after Pearl Harbor. How handsome Rob was in his navy blue sailor's uniform. And now, in the quiet aftermath of daily routine, it is still something to think about and savor, as she does her nightly chores.

"How was the old lady?" asks Rob, as he stirs his coffee. He doesn't really care about the answer; it's just to make conversation. Betty knows he doesn't want her to work. And so she is careful not to tell

BETTEJANE SYNOTT WESSON

him anything bad about her days at Chrysanthemum Lodge with Lady Muck, as her mother-in-law calls the woman she has never met.

"Lunch was a nice chicken salad," she says, knowing that Rob hates salad. It's a little thing, a way not to make the job sound too good for fear of seeming to compare the two worlds and find theirs lacking. Betty's dishes, underneath the evening's pork chops, are white with red roses at the centers and gold rims, set on a white linen cloth with a border of little Dutch girls with tulip bouquets.

"Why go to the trouble of ironing?" asks Cora, who feels that a table unadorned is fine for every day use.

"Because it's elegant," Betty replies. Elegant, to her, is the best that anything can be. It has led her as far afield as the Wedding Embassy's annual sale of leftover dresses in flower-girl size for Betts to play dress up.

After supper and her bath, firmly tucked into bed, Betts falls asleep, listening to her parents' voices in the kitchen. The light from the room just around the corner streams across her bedroom threshold. Her stuffed cats and teddy bears are lined up beside her. The small gray house is snug in the cool March night. And next day, Betty's job goes on.

"Nurse! Bring me my lipstick," Mrs. Goodly commands. Revlon's Love that Red is her preferred color.

"And a hand mirror. And my blue negligee." Dr. Griswold is making his weekly house call to the invalid, and Mrs. Goodly insists on looking her best. She has spent the better part of an hour this morning instructing Euphonia on cutting the stems from a bouquet of roses so they can be floated in a bowl of water. The bowl is Baccarat. The pink roses are brown edged, wilted to a point of no return.

"Remember, girls, that this is a good housekeeper's thrifty way to get the most from one's blossoms," their employer says. Betty and Euphonia roll their eyes at each other behind her back. Euphonia stifles a giggle.

When the doctor arrives, he inquires about his charge.

"Oh, about the same," Betty reports. She does not mention the nasty bits involved in caring for Elvira Goodly, for example the sly way she has of storing up her gas to expel in her nurse's face when she demands to be rolled onto her side.

"Oopsie," she'll say with a laugh.

"Ah, the pain, Doctor," she begins as the doctor enters, in the elaborate pas de deux ballet they dance that ensures a plentiful supply of her drug. Before she fell down the main staircase one evening after one nightcap too many, Mrs. Goodly was what some textbooks once called a dipsomaniac. But bed rest recovery from her bruises brought morphine into the picture, and now she far prefers it to her old friend Gilbey's gin.

"By the way," Dr. Griswold tells Betty as he hands her the latest prescription, "something big fell off the roof as I was coming in."

She walks him to the door and looks out. It is one of the winged stone gargoyles that guard the downspouts on the four corners of the porte cochere. It lies belly up in the gravel, grinning. *How heavy it is,* she thinks, as she moves it out of the drive into a weedy flower bed.

"And there he'll be forever unless he sprouts a pair of legs," Euphonia tells her, "with no gardener around any more to put him back up high."

It's just one more thing on a list of things that strike Betty as odd. Why gargoyles in the first place? She wonders. It is as much a puzzle to her as the long-departed Mr. Goodly's rubber waders that still hang in the master bathroom on a hook behind the door. They are olive green, chest high, with suspenders and built-in boots at the bottoms of the legs. The big white tub is deep, and Betty imagines Mr. Goodly stepping into it to test the water tight capacity of his sports regalia. On his dressing room wall above a cupboard filled with yellowed dress shirts, there is a big spotty mounted fish with glass eyes. Mrs. Goodly is only too glad to tell Betty about the wily brook trout her late husband captured on opening day of fishing in 1922.

"That is a prime example of the speckled trout found in northeast Quebec, my dear, preserved by the taxidermist with its mouth open to suggest it is at rest in the water."

Betty sees the dead fish as just one more clue to how the rich are different. The twenty-odd-roomed mansion and its glass conservatory filled with dead plants are full of clues, she thinks. Betty imagines herself as a sleuth like Lamont Cranston, man about town, who is really the Shadow, on the track of one of his weekly radio mysteries.

What she hopes to find out is how exactly to climb a step higher in Waterbury's class system. It's not so much for her but for Betts. Betty wants to figure out what makes rich people tick. Why they think they are better than everybody else.

And so when Elvira Goodly begins one of her narratives with "When I was a girl," Betty listens for something that may come in handy down the road.

She wonders how you would get to be like them. So elegant. Cocksure. She never asks herself why you'd want to in the first place.

"Johnny jump-ups" is what her Irish family calls social climbers. There is a difference as wide as the Atlantic Ocean between them and the folks her family designate as "born with a silver spoon in their mouths," a group that includes Betty's employer.

Making a distinction between jump-ups and people who simply want to better themselves, "I'll do as I please," Betty tells her reflection in the long mirror as she dons her raincoat in the huge drafty entrance hall of Chrysanthemum Lodge. It's nearly April. Easter is late this year, and there has been speculation at home as to whether she will receive a bonus for the holiday. Betty wasn't on the job yet at Christmastime, but she has heard that the previous nurses were given fruit cakes. She hates fruit cakes and considers that she has dodged a bullet in the gift department.

Her neighbor Mrs. O'Leary served her some once. She and her neighbor just two doors down on Willow Street on the first floor of a massive triple-decker house have become friends. Betty often stops in on her way back up the hill to check and see if the elderly widow needs anything.

"Sit," she'll urge, "and have a cup of tea." Betty hates tea with a passion, having been raised on inky black pots of it morning, noon, and night. But with equally intense passion, she longs for Mrs. O'Leary's tea cart. Golden oak with a glass tray top that detaches so it can be carried by its curved handles, it gleams in the sunny bow window of her neighbor's dining room.

"I'll give it to you, one day," her neighbor tells her. Betty imagines the cart in her own living room with a doily on top and perhaps her prized Hummel figurine of the Happy Wanderer.

Mrs. O'Leary is about the age of Elvira Goodly. And both have lived in their respective houses for decades. In Mrs. Goodly's case, she'd come as a bride to her husband's ancestral home. In Mrs. O'Leary's, her yellow house was built by her father. The only things the two houses have in common are their bulk and their age. It is the contrast between the two women, also of the same age, that interests Betty. Her neighbor's lace curtains are freshly laundered, her wedding china in daily use. The porch is swept, the front lawn cut.

This is what she's familiar with, this "taking care of your things," as her mother would say. Mrs. O'Leary's situation is still a step up for Betty, but it's a manageable step. Of course there is always more to a story than there seems at first glance, and Betty's mother is the back story to Betty's aspirations. Zora Keane has "come from something" over there in Ireland, as she often reminds her daughter.

On Zora's bureau is a heavy silver-backed mirror, comb, and brush set, its elaborate monogrammed *Z* ending in a curlicue of shamrocks.

And in the parlor, a whatnot shelf boasts a Waterford glass pitcher and an ornamental mother-of-pearl fish with a transfer picture of Ross Castle, its top hollowed out for tiny shakers of salt and pepper. These bits of elegance point to a past quite different from her current one in Waterbury. When Betty was small, she'd discovered that her mother's choice of a husband was what had changed the course of her history, and that the impediment to Zora's return was Betty herself.

Being made to feel that she has kept her mother from reclaiming what seems to have been a bed-of-roses existence has been quite a burden for Betty to carry all these years, and it motivates her even now to try and get back for herself a bit of what she feels was lost.

"Don't hold out hope for a bonus," Zora tells Betty. "The rich did not become so by giving their money away."

"I won't, Mam," Betty replies, though she can't help dreaming a bit of what she'd do with a windfall.

It's the first day of April, and spring is in the air. Betty helps her employer into a fresh nightgown and raises the bedroom shades.

"You Catholics must be eager to put an end to your penances," she remarks, referring to Betty's observance of Lent that includes meatless Friday meals. "It has been a great deal of trouble for Cook to accommodate you, my dear."

Cook is the third generation of her family employed in this household and has regaled Betty and all the staff with stories of how the original Mrs. Goodly, creator of the mansion, always demanded early breakfast in bed on Sunday mornings to prevent Cook's mother from walking the uphill mile to Saint Margaret's mission church for Mass.

Saint Margaret's on Willow Street is Betty's church as well. Betts is set to make her first Holy Communion there next month in a white dress and veil. For Easter Sunday, Betty has gotten them matching straw hats with tiny multicolored flowers. Mother-daughter outfits are big this year. For herself, there is a new gray suit with a silk flower corsage. They are a handsome, happy family, she thinks, and on Easter, they will look the part.

Looking and being are practically the same thing, as Betty sees it. She is glad for Rob in her family picture. His steadiness anchors her. She wonders if it is the man that makes the lady. She thinks of the late Mr. Goodly, reduced now to a pair of waders in the master bath. Of her father driving his rusty black Ford across town to collect her mother after a visit. Of Rob at the day's end in the kitchen rocker, reading the newspaper. Surely not, she tells herself.

Betty believes that, although money has its say, it is the woman with imagination and grit who has the last word.

It is thanks to herself that they own a home, with the dishes she dreamed of as a girl on her own pantry shelves, and that she herself has a profession rather than a lackluster job. Betty remembers something she learned in grammar school, one of those things the nuns made you memorize. The nuns at Saint Mary's were great for that. Usually it was blather, the kind of verbal puzzle that they'd use to confuse you.

"To travel hopefully is better than to arrive," she'd learned, but she'd thought them mad for saying it. She'd favored the arrival at her destination over the journey every time. But now? She is not so sure. This morning, her patient has been animated by the arrival of the mail. There are Easter cards, five of them, from her children, bearing out-of-state return addresses.

"They never forget their mother," she tells Betty, who privately thinks, *And they never show up here either.*

"All this will be theirs someday," Mrs. Goodly adds, with a gesture that includes the dusty drapes, the crumbling house, and its down at heel neighborhood. It's abundantly clear that Betty's employer hasn't left her bedroom for a number of years.

"I'm glad I'm young," she tells Euphonia. "And I'm glad that Betts is small." She thinks of cuddling at night before tucking her in and of their plans when school is over to go to the Bronx Zoo. She finds it delicious to anticipate all the good times yet to come.

"Me too. And I'm sure glad I'm not that old lady," Euphonia replies. "She gave me my Easter present this morning. 'Here is a crisp, new five-dollar bill for you,' she said. 'You may use it to buy your holiday dinner.'"

"Well," Betty tells her, "smoked ham is on sale at fifty-eight cents a pound this week at the A&P. How many people are you planning to feed?"

"It's for sure that Lady Bountiful hasn't been grocery shopping in a month of Sundays," Euphonia replies with a laugh that ends in a snort. "I'll put her Easter contribution toward my desserts."

In the yard by the porte cochere, daffodils have suddenly sprung up in no apparent order, nearly obscuring the deposed gargoyle. That's one of the nice things about spring, Betty thinks. The surprises. Readying her employer for the evening shift, she is surprised yet again when Mrs. Goodly reaches out a jeweled, blue-veined claw and takes her wrist.

"Nurse," she begins, "I have a small token of my esteem for you. Open the top drawer of my mirrored bureau." Betty does so, gazing into a welter of castoff objects: empty powder compacts, old lipsticks, letters, and a few handkerchiefs monogrammed in blue.

"You may select a handkerchief."

"But Mrs. Goodly, these are all monogrammed with your initial."

"It is yours, as well, my dear, if Betty is indeed still the diminutive for Elizabeth."

The handkerchiefs are yellowed, some with little oval gold stickers still in place that read, "Made in Switzerland." Mrs. Goodly interprets Betty's silence as awe.

"A lady always carries a linen handkerchief, my dear. Elegance cannot be compromised."

Betty laughs uneasily. *Could this be an April Fool's Day joke?* She thinks.

Her employer waits expectantly for thanks.

"A Happy Easter to you, Nurse. I'll take my morphine now. After that, you may be on your way. No doubt you have things to do at home for your holiday preparations."

"How'd you make out?" Euphonia asks, as Betty comes down the stairs.

Wordlessly, she waves the hankie.

"Oh, honey, 'them that has, gets,' as my mother used to say," Euphonia laughs. It's exactly what Betty needs to put the scene into perspective. She laughs too, but this time with conviction.

It's warmed up quite a bit since she left for work this morning, and Betty unbuttons her coat. She puts her gloves into her pockets as she turns the corner to Willow Street and feels the handkerchief.

"Jesus!" she says out loud. "The rich are different, all right." Beginning to fashion the incident into a story to tell to her family at supper, she anticipates their laughter. Betty hurries up the little sidewalk that leads to her green front door. Ladylike or not, as she opens it, she shouts, "I'm home!"

LITTLE DOLLS

The Christmas morning that I found the dollhouse underneath our tree I was still my parents' only child. I'd picked the shiny two-story tin colonial out of our Sears Catalogue and put it on my wish list for Santa. I no longer believed that Santa was real. But my parents clearly did, and I hated to disappoint them. My mother had been glum for a while. I didn't know why. I'd heard her tell Dad that her doctor had told her to relax, things happened when you weren't expecting them. Dad asked if the doctor had been making a joke.

Shortly afterward, my weekend routine changed, and I began to cross town every Friday night to spend the weekend with Mom's parents. My grandfather's rusty black Ford with running boards pulled alongside the curb in front of our house each Friday night at five.

"On the money again," he'd remark, sending sparks from his cigarette. They'd fall like little stars into the soapy water pooled in the hollows of our front steps from their daily washing. Grandpa rolled his own smokes each Saturday, packing tobacco from the dented canister stored behind the couch into tissue-thin papers that he sealed shut with his tongue.

Aligned like crooked soldiers, they marched across the kitchen table as Grandma set the dishes out for tea. I'd watch him roll the crumbly tobacco, fabricating stories with equal dexterity from daily events of a life that most would call prosaic.

"Tell about when you fought the Black and Tans," I'd urge. "Tell about the crossroad dances where you met Grandma."

"Too many stories are bad for a child," my grandmother remarked after I'd picked up on something they'd said when they thought I wasn't listening. To change the subject, she asked if I'd my dollhouse to be brought over along with me on my next visit so I could play with it all weekend.

The dollhouse had come without tenants, but its brightly colored plastic furniture and little rooms with stamped pictures of plants and books on its walls were so absorbing that I hardly noticed their absence. I pretended I was tiny enough to fit into the rooms, and peopled it myself, with my imagination.

"You ought to have dolls for your nursery," said Grandma, and returned from her foray to Woolworth's with three little pink plastic people.

"They look cold," Dad's mother observed, wiggling their tiny, articulated arms and legs. "I'll crochet them some dresses and bonnets."

My mother seemed indifferent to my dollhouse. But one Sunday afternoon when she came to collect me, I noticed her staring at its nursery, a pink and blue room where smiling lambs capered above a dado of alphabet letters on its shiny lithographed walls.

"Look, the wheels on the baby carriage move," I showed her.

"Yours is stored in our attic," she replied.

As I pushed my own carriage along the kitchen table, Grandma said, "Those dolls are too big for it, you need a tiny one." The one she chose from Woolworth's arrived soon afterward in a little pink plastic cradle, held firmly in place by a rubber band. I found that it changed the dynamic in my house. The parent dolls were up in their yellow bedroom. The third doll was in its nursery. But where did the fourth one fit in?

"Put her in the nursery too," suggested Grandma, so I did. But the new arrangement looked makeshift. The change made me uneasy.

On my next visit, Grandma surprised me with a magical present, a cellophane packet labeled Moon Rocks. No doubt the gift was intended to sweeten the fact that my mother was leaving me at my grandparents for an entire week while she went on a trip. Together, Grandma and I set the garishly colored lumps in the bottom of an empty milk bottle, added the cloudy solution that we mixed as directed, and went to bed.

Next morning we saw that the rocks had begun to grow into stalagmites of blue and yellow, magenta and lime. They seemed like a miracle to me, something seemingly impossible yet true. My mother was expecting a miracle of her own at the end of her trip. She'd gone to Canada by train, taking Dad's mother along as a translator fluent in French.

I knew Canada from *The Early Show* movies on TV as a country filled with mounted police in red jackets who befriended Shirley Temple and sang love songs to Jeanette MacDonald. But these glimpses of the vast country to our north did not include the place my mother was going. Her destination was the Shrine of Saint Anne de Beaupre. The Mother of the Blessed Virgin Mary, Saint Anne was also Jesus' grandmother. Babies were her specialty, and my mother's pilgrimage was to ask for one.

"Be good," Mom said as she kissed me good-bye. She was wearing lipstick and high heels with her Sunday suit, so I knew this was an occasion. It was Friday again, the day when Catholics lived dangerously, since the pope forbade us to eat meat. We substituted fish, glistening fillets that Grandma dipped in flour to fry. They had bones so tiny that they looked like threads.

"Chew carefully," Grandma admonished. "These bones could choke you to death."

"Don't frighten her, woman," said Grandpa. "We're safe. We've been blessed by Saint Blaise." He was referring to the night each February when Catholics went to church to have their throats blessed by a priest holding crossed candlesticks. It was a great thing to be in with the saints as friends, I thought, as long as your petitions to them came back answered yes.

After dinner, Grandma and I walked over to the vacant lot across from her front door. I thought of it as the woods, overgrown as it was with saplings and a tangle of bittersweet. In the clearing was a maple tree so tall that my head rested on the back of my shoulders when I tried to see its top. The tree dropped seeds paired like tiny angels' wings, joined at the center where the stem met the rounded bulbs that held the future plant. I slit one open with my fingernail to look inside, but the tree held its mystery of creation, or else I lacked the knowledge to interpret what I'd found.

I collected a handful of its fallen leaves and bundled them into the hollow at the tree's base. I added a few twigs on top for logs, the bright leaves beneath them for the fire.

"You've a grand hearth there," said Grandma. I thought about my mother so far away in Canada and shivered.

"We'd better go in if you're cold," she told me. The last of the sun made an orange curtain behind her head.

"A good night for a story," Grandpa observed, booting Sparky, the runty tabby cat I'd named, out the door. He pulled the shade, adding a scoop of coal from the bin in the furnace room. I could see the fire through the grate in the furnace door. The flames lapped the black lumps like bright little tongues. The kitchen grew as warm as a pair of Christmas slippers. The table lay between us like an empty stage. I leaned forward on my elbows, a picture of rapt attention. Grandpa's stories brimmed with opportunities for disclosure if the audience was right. Safe from Grandma's disapproval, since she'd gone upstairs, he began.

It was a rescue story, my grandfather the hero as usual. This time he'd rescued Grandma's cat from drowning.

"He was going down for the third time when into the lake I dove, without hesitation."

I longed for details. Did he remove his shoes first? What was the name of the cat? But I'd learned that interruptions could prove fatal to the story line, so I kept quiet.

"Herself and I locked eyes. And that was that for us." I studied him through the smoky haze of his cigarette as he added, "Fate. You can't beat it."

Fate presented a completely different angle on life from saints and prayers, and it worried me. I pictured it as a giant hand reaching down to move us around the way I did my dolls and furniture when I reached into my dollhouse. And later, lying in bed, listening to the clock strike the hours, I took care to keep my back against the wall in case fate might be reaching down for me.

My mother surprised me next morning, coming in the front door as I was finishing my egg and toast.

"I've brought you a surprise," she said, handing me a box. I untied the string and unwrapped the brown paper. Inside the long, narrow box lay a doll that looked a lot like me. I touched her wavy red hair.

"It's human hair," said Mom, and so were the eyelashes that fringed her blue glass eyes. The doll was dressed in a tartan kilt and a jaunty cocked hat. At her waist hung a little fur purse that my mother told me was called a sporran.

"What will you name her?" asked Grandma. "She's enough like you to be your sister."

"And may well be the only one she'll ever have," Mom replied, her voice at odds with her smile.

"I'll call her the Scotch Doll," I told them, eager to fill the silence with words. When I laid her on her back in her box her eyes clicked slowly shut.

I didn't care to play with my new doll. I sensed in her a reticence equal to my own.

"She's so special that I'll keep her for show," I said, knowing it would please my mother that I agreed with her philosophy that some things were just too nice to use.

To change the subject, I continued, "Tell about how Grandpa rescued your cat back in Ireland, Grandma, and you knew he was your fate."

With a noise that was almost like a gasp, Grandma said, "The moxie of him, telling such nonsense to a child! It's just another one of his stories. Don't believe a word he said."

What a relief it was to me to hear fate dethroned, and the story dismissed as a whopper. Without fate, there was a chance for people to have things go the way they'd like them to. Still, Grandpa's stories were magic. For example, I knew that the glass slippers like Cinderella's that he'd ordered me were still at the shoemaker's awaiting their final touches. And the pony he'd promised was only on hold until the grass in our backyard grew long enough for it to graze. The way my grandfather tried to grant my every wish was as good as having my own personal saint.

That night, I slept at home in my own bed, my new doll staring blank faced from her bureau pedestal.

"Did you say your prayers?" Mom asked when she came to tuck me in. I had.

"Me too," she told me, looking at my doll.

Across town, my dollhouse sat in the living room of my grandparents' house, the little dolls asleep too in their plastic beds, awaiting my return. We were all of us waiting for something, whether it would come by magic or fate or prayer.

"Sweet dreams," my mother whispered as she turned out the light.

AH, FRESH AIR

Cora folds the morning *Republican* and sets it down on the table. It's a hot morning in early August, and she has been reading in the paper about an organization called the Fresh Air Fund that sends inner city children to the country for a refreshing change of pace. Her granddaughters are out on the front porch, reading their latest stack of library books under the green awning's deep shade and well aware of being only two houses away from Dave's Superette and its big glass cases filled with frosty ice cream bars and Coke.

They haven't complained about summer in the city, but the newspaper's account of the joys of country life have gotten Cora to thinking about her own girlhood up in Massachusetts, in a town rural enough for her family to have had chickens and goats.

Cora lifts the heavy receiver of the black desk phone on her kitchen counter and makes a call. She has a big family, and one of her brothers has a cottage on a lake.

"We're going to get some fresh country air this Sunday," she announces to Betts and Molly and later to their parents as well as to her husband, Mike.

"Oh, brother," Rob tells his wife. He prefers his mother's family at a safe distance.

"Well, it would be nice to cool off in a lake," Betty replies. She is remembering her Sunday excursions to Scovill's Dam back when she was Betts's age.

"Maybe we'll see cows on our way there," Molly says. Molly likes cows, especially the black and white ones. When they take a Sunday ride, if they see cows, her mother makes a game of naming them.

"Hello, Genevieve," she'll call, pretending one is their neighbor. "Hello, Aunt Carol. Hello, Aunt Maureen." As often as Betty does this, the girls still convulse in laughter at her daring.

"How far away is this place?" Mike asks.

"Not so far," Cora tells him. "It's in Bethlehem."

"It's in the town where Baby Jesus was born?" asks Molly, who has learned the Christmas carol about Bethlehem in school.

"No, silly," Betty tells her. "This Bethlehem is here in Connecticut. We can be there in under an hour."

"Let's all go in one car," Mike says.

"I'll get the map out of my glove compartment," Rob offers.

Even though the actual distance from Waterbury to Benson Grove can be measured in minutes, it fails to factor in the time warp of going from cement sidewalks and window boxes full of tidy geraniums to a place where nature silently does whatever it pleases.

"It looks like the jungle in a Tarzan movie here," Betts reports, peering out the open window in the hot breeze.

Mike's car turns left off Route 61 and onto a dirt road. The entrance to the enclave of cottages is marked by a wooden sign that reads, "Welcome to Benson Grove." The sign looks hand lettered, and beneath the words is a tiny log cabin silhouetted in hunter green. Green smoke curls from the cabin's chimney, twisting back on itself like a finger crooked as if to say, "Come in."

"Look! The lake!" says Molly. The little lake is the reason for Benson Grove's existence. Its water looks almost black in the shade from the towering hemlock trees around it, cool and inviting. Betty shifts in the backseat, her feet planted on either side of a dozen ears of corn and a bouquet of pink gladioli they have purchased as a hostess gift along the way from a roadside stand.

"We're here," says Mike, pulling up on the grass in front of a tan cottage.

"Jesus, this place is the size of a bread box," Rob answers.

"Shush," Cora tells him. "I see my brother Ellard."

"Welcome, all," calls Ellard from the front steps. He is dressed in khaki trousers held up by red suspenders and a sleeveless undershirt. It's the type of undershirt Rob calls a wife beater, but he keeps this observation to himself.

"We brought corn," Cora tells him.

"Oh, boy, then I hope you are ready to shuck it yourselves," Ellard replies. "Mimi hates that job."

Ellard's wife joins him on the steps. Cora offers her the flowers.

"Gee, I don't know what I will put them in," Mimi says.

"No problem, dear. We can use a bucket," says Ellard.

While the grown-ups are talking, Molly and Betts are looking around. Squirrels are chasing each other through the trees above them, and something is rustling in the underbrush. But the most amazing sight to them is the vines. They have been hacked back from the small side lawn to make way for a badminton net, but it is plain to see that the vines want in.

"If we play and the shuttlecock goes in the thicket, I am not going after it," Betts tells Molly. "Who knows what might be in there?"

"Why don't you all change, and we'll go for a swim," Ellard suggests, leading the way up the steps through the front door.

"Mimi's niece is here," he continues, gesturing to a girl a little older than Betts. She is sitting on the couch with her left index finger knuckle deep into a stick of butter. She is holding the butter dish with her right hand. Betts can see the toast crumbs stuck onto the plate.

"I burned myself making popcorn," she says. "I'm Marlene."

The swimming area is a short walk from the cottage, and they set off, Rob carrying his US Navy blanket, and Mike, the beach umbrella. Molly is wearing rubber beach shoes from the Uniroyal outlet shop in Naugatuck. Molly does not like to step on pebbles in her bare feet.

"Last one in is a rotten egg," calls Marlene, stroking out to the raft where she lies sunning. Betts thinks she looks like a seal in a *National Geographic* magazine but tells herself she may just be jealous because her Red Cross swimming lessons at the Crosby High School pool have left her terrified of water.

"Go on in, why don't you?" Mimi urges her. "The water is fine. Unless, of course, you think you are too good for our lake."

Betts responds to her mother's warning look and wades out. The plaid skirt of her bathing suit fans out around her in the water, and so she does not see Marlene swim up behind her. Suddenly Betts finds herself underwater, a hand around her ankles and her eyes level with the lake's sandy bottom. She sees a pair of feet with chipped red toenail polish and realizes what has happened. She'd scream, but that would fill her mouth with water. Betts struggles and the hand on her ankles lets go.

"Gotcha, you big baby!" says Marlene. Ellard waves at them from shore. "I love to see kids enjoying themselves," he tells the folks on the blanket.

Betty has swum far out, to cool off both from the heat and from her wrath over Mimi's remark that she has put on a few pounds since the last time they met.

"Let it go, you're gorgeous," Rob told her, so she tries, but she'd like to tell Mimi that she has a lot of nerve. Cora has unfortunately forgotten to apply the Coppertone suntan lotion and is turning a rosy shade of pink. Molly comes up to the blanket with a handful of pebbles she has been collecting, round white ones, some with a touch of mica.

"I think they're magic rocks," she tells her grandfather. Mike agrees and puts them in his bathing suit pocket for safekeeping.

On the way back to the cottage, the girls are invited to pick blackberries in the neighbor's yard. The berries are huge and juicy and, despite the bramble scratches they get and the mosquito bites, well worth it. The neighbor's grown-up daughter, a heavy dark-haired woman with a yappy little lap dog, watches silently from her wheelchair on the porch.

"You know, girls," Mimi tells them as they wash the berries in the kitchen sink, "that poor cripple, Gloria, used to be a regular little girl just like you. One summer day she went swimming in the lake as usual, and she went to bed at night, and next day she woke up paralyzed from polio. Imagine that. She could not move a muscle ever again."

Marlene takes the story in stride, and fortunately Molly has left the room, but Betts is terrified. She has just witnessed firsthand the randomness of life thanks to Marlene's water grab, and now she is on edge, waiting for the next bad thing to happen.

In the living room, Betty is applying Noxema to Cora's sunburn and giving dirty looks to Mimi's back. Rob and his father signal to each other to go outside for a bit.

"How about a game of badminton before supper?" says Mike.

"This looks to me like a good time to take these little gals here for a boat ride," Ellard tells them.

Betts tries to beg off, but Betty tells her, "Go on and get in the boat. I need you to keep an eye on your little sister."

Betts dreads returning to the lake, but when they follow Ellard across the street to the neighbor's dock, she is suddenly glad to have come along. Although it's shady beneath the pines, Ellard's boat is in the sunlight, sparkling like a beautiful toy. It's a wooden boat, freshly varnished to the color of wild honey. The boat's leather cushions are red, piped in white. The steering wheel is white too, and the boat's logo, Chris-Craft, is spelled out in gleaming chrome.

Mimi is written on the stern in big gold block letters. Ellard holds out his hand.

"Climb in, gals," he says, and they do, one at a time, squealing a little as the boat rocks beneath their weight.

Betts studies the houses on shore as they circle the lake. Unlike their uniform plain fronts, the sides that face the lake all have secrets that can only be discovered from the water. Some have flagpoles and white Adirondack chairs. Many have wide screened porches or striped hammocks. And one red cottage made of logs like a pioneer's cabin has a weathervane of an Indian paddling a canoe. The lake water is so clear that Betts can see the grasses swaying on the bottom and make out the dark shapes of the occasional fish swimming by. She'd like to trail her hand in the boat's wake the way Marlene is doing, but she is held back by the fear that something might pull her under.

Ellard cuts the outboard engine at the center of the lake, and they drift.

"Wanna fish?" he asks Molly, producing a pole and a lure from the boat's locker beneath the driver's seat.

"Oh!" says Molly. She is captivated by the glistening silver lure with blue and yellow feathers on its end to hide the hook.

"The fish get hungry in the late afternoon," Ellard tells her. And it is not long at all before her pole bends beneath the weight of her first ever catch. It's a small trout, and Molly decides to put him back.

"His mother will miss him," she says. Marlene laughs, but Betts can tell that Ellard approves of her decision.

"You can catch him again next time," he tells her. Betts hopes there will not be a next time, but Molly is happy to hear it.

Back at the cottage, Cora is out in the yard, whispering to Mike about Mimi's rudeness over the hostess gifts of flowers and corn. Mike is laughing out loud. He is getting a kick out of the day.

"You tell her, Cora. I'll hold the baby," he says. It's one of his favorite expressions. "Today was your idea," he reminds her. He knows he shouldn't rub it in, but he says it anyway.

"Well, I only came here for the girls," Cora sniffs. She begins to shuck the corn.

The cookout supper has ended, and the family is sitting around the picnic table in the backyard. Betts is swatting at mosquitoes, and Rob is wondering if he will ever be able to digest Ellard's brand of hot dog. It seems to be stuck somewhere in his chest.

"I hate to go, but I guess it's time," Cora begins.

"Oh no," says Mimi. "Not yet. Marlene is going to entertain us on her banjo." It's a brown plastic instrument one grade up from a carnival toy, but Marlene plunks it with determination as she sings:

"Shine on, shine on harvest moon, up in the sky.

I ain't had no loving since January, February, June, or July."

Betty, looking at chubby Marlene with her stringy hair, thinks she can understand why. Betts is horrified to hear a song with the word "ain't" used instead of "have not."

"I wasn't expecting Ted Mack and his *Original Amateur Hour*," Rob whispers to Betty. They laugh together quietly as they bend beneath the picnic table out of the breeze to light their cigarettes.

But Molly likes the song. She is sitting on the bottom step of the cottage. It is made of cement, and it is still warm from the sun. Molly has retrieved her magic pebbles from Mike's pocket and is counting them. There are six, a nice even number to hold, three in each hand.

Everyone claps politely when Marlene is finished, and they stand up quickly to prevent an encore.

"Come again," calls Ellard as their car backs down the lawn and turns into the road.

The grown-ups have changed seats for the ride home. Rob is in front with Mike, riding shotgun. Molly is between them. In the backseat, Cora and Betty flank Betts.

"Well, that was hell," Betty says.

"To heck with getting any more fresh country air," Cora adds.

"For Pete's sake, girls, lighten up," Mike tells them. As a doughboy who spent the Great War in France crawling on his belly through the mud of no-man's-land, he cannot find one thing wrong with a summer afternoon of swimming and picnicking and shade.

"I'm just saying," Cora begins. "I'm just saying that none of us had a good time."

Betts and Betty nod in agreement, but then from the front seat Molly says, "I caught a little fish, and I had a ride in a boat. And I found some magic rocks. Today was the best day of my life."

The sun is setting behind Mike's car as they head east toward Waterbury and home. The sky is red and orange behind them, and its intense golden light turns the towering pines at the entrance to Benson Grove into black sentinels. Cora and Betty have exchanged glances and decided to say no more about the day until there are just the two of them. But after Molly's comment, Betty turns to Cora and whispers, pointing to Molly, "I don't know where that one came from."

"The angels, maybe," she continues. "Or the fairies, as they'd say in Ireland."

Molly doesn't hear her mother, though. She is busy examining her magic rocks to see which one is the best. They all are, she thinks. Each and every one deserves a prize.

DODO

Betty does not have very much to do with her neighbors beyond what her husband jokingly calls her hello-good-bye routine. Willow Street is changing around them. Families are moving out to new little ranch houses on the far sides of the city. Her daughter Betts's best friend from the apartment building on the corner has left town entirely and moved with her parents to Cheshire. It's the way things are going in the inner part of the city in 1958.

But across the busy street a new family has just arrived.

"That is Mary Doreen Dougherty, by the look of her," says Betty's mother. "Your father and I know her family from Sunday Mass." Zora's parish is a big one on the east side of town. It boasts its own grammar school, convent, high school, and rectory, in addition to a large red brick house of worship.

Mary Doreen is slender, with pale skin and watery blue eyes. Her hair is the color of cocoa added to milk with a stingy hand. On this morning, she is supervising a moving van, and her third finger, left hand, sports a modest diamond and a gold wedding band as she points the way for the movers into the first floor rent.

"Mary Doreen, is that you?" calls Zora from Betty's front porch.

"Oh, Mrs. Finn! Hello! I'm Mrs. Mike Kajak now. I'm married."

"Come over for a cup of tea when the movers go," Betty says. She puts the kettle on and gets out a package of chocolate chips. It's summer vacation, and so Betts joins the ladies. Mary Doreen tells them about how she almost went off to art school after she got her high school diploma.

"But I met Mike. And that was that," she laughs.

With a baby on the way, Mary Doreen has plans for painting a mural on its nursery walls.

"Come and visit me," she tells Betts. "You can help me pick out the nursery rhymes for Mike Junior's pictures. I think I'll begin with 'the cow jumped over the moon.'" When she says good-bye, she kisses Zora and shakes Betty's hand.

"All my friends call me Dodo," she says. "And you must call me Dodo too."

"A pity that she did not stay in school," Zora tells Betty. "Mary Doreen had a scholarship to college. Her artwork was that good."

They move back to the front porch, and when the five-thirty bus comes up the hill, a strange new man gets off, a man in work clothes.

"That must be Mary Doreen's husband, by the cut of him. She did tell us that he works in a garage."

"She said to call her Dodo, Grandma," Betts reminds her.

"I'd rather a different name for her, that one has a funny connotation."

Betts gets out their *Consolidated Webster Dictionary* and looks the word up. "Dodo," she reads, "is a large, clumsy bird now extinct. Covered with down, its short wings and tail are useless for flight. A second meaning for the word is silly or foolish." She cannot see how either definition could apply to their new neighbor.

"Betts, honey, read the rhyme to me again, will you?"

Betts and Dodo are in what will be the baby's room. It's on the south side of the rent and sunny. Dodo is perched on a step stool. She's sketching the outline of the mural.

Hey, diddle, diddle,
The cat and the fiddle,
The cow jumped over the moon;
The little dog laughed
To see such sport,
And the dish ran away with the spoon.

Betts watches as a laughing cow emerges from Dodo's pencil tip. It jumps over a smiling moon that Dodo says will be painted chartreuse.

"Because the moon is made of green cheese, or so they say," she tells Betts.

There is a long-whiskered white cat on another wall, playing a violin, a little Scottie dog that looks as if he's just heard a good joke, and a big plate with stars in its border, dancing hand in hand with a serving spoon. It's an interpretation of the Mother Goose rhyme that will delight any baby, Betts thinks. She almost wishes it was in her own room.

And she is not the only one who is enchanted. As family and neighbors see the completed work, they ask Dodo to go to their house to paint. And pretty soon, she has a cottage industry going.

"You should have business cards made," Betty tells her.

"I've put up a little sign at the corner grocery," Dodo replies. "That's enough advertising for now, with the baby due next month."

Dodo's latest commissions include the waiting room of her baby's future pediatrician and the nursery of a Hillside mansion where the fairy tale characters are all to have captions beneath them in French.

"Oh la la," Betty says.

"Well, I like to give them what they want," says Dodo.

"Does your husband mind?"

"Mike doesn't care as long as his dinner is on time. Besides, the money I'm making goes into our bank account for a rainy day."

Her laughter makes it clear that Dodo thinks such a day will never come.

Little Mike Junior arrives and is duly christened. Father Reilly tells the family and their friends what a gift a new soul is.

"May you have many more," he adds.

"It looks as if Dodo took that suggestion to heart," Betty tells her mother. "She's pregnant again, and this time it's with twins."

Dodo keeps on painting. Little Mike Junior goes along in his baby carriage, her paints and sable-tipped brushes stored beneath his seat.

"My varicose veins are killing me," says Dodo. "But of course, it's worth it. As Father Reilly says, babies are a gift to us from God."

It's winter when the twins are born. Betty goes across the street one day to check up on the family and finds Dodo crying.

"I don't know what to do first," she explains. All three babies are howling. There's a mound of dirty diapers in the bathtub and rows of bottles waiting to be filled with formula lined up on the counter by the kitchen sink.

"I haven't combed my hair in days," Dodo says. "In fact, I'm not even sure what day of the week today is." Betty tells her to lie down and brings her a cup of tea. She tidies the place, settles the babies, and breathes a sigh of relief to return to her own spotless home.

"Mom, there's a police car across the street," Betts reports the next afternoon as she returns from school. An ambulance soon follows, its banshee siren heralding its arrival.

"Mary Doreen was not feeling quite herself," Dodo's mother tells Betty. "She has gone away for a little rest."

Word spreads fast through the neighborhood that Dodo was found unresponsive in her kitchen when the upstairs neighbor knocked, driven nearly mad by the sound of the screaming babies. Dodo was in a kitchen chair with her head resting on the open oven door. Her pink apron was over her head, the gas stove on but its pilot light extinguished.

When Mary Doreen returns from Saint Mary's Hospital, Betty goes across the street with a cake. The three babies are as quiet as dolls under Mrs. Dougherty's firm hand, and as the tea is poured, Betty learns about Father Reilly's visit.

"He told me that what I did was a mortal sin. He said that suicide flies in the face of the Fifth Commandment, 'Thou shall not kill.' And of course it was beyond selfish of me to try to leave Mike and the babies."

Betty can see by Dodo's occasional lightheadedness and the twitching of one eye that she is suffering the after effects of the Thorazine she was given.

"But they took me off it when they discovered that I was expecting."

"Mary Doreen, have you never heard of family planning?" Betty asks.

"Sure. At the Cana Conference Mike and I went to before we married. 'Abstinence? Yes. Contraception? No,'" she quotes. "They told us that 'though it is challenging for Catholics to balance affection and restraint, it can be done with discipline and prayer.'"

"I'm leaving now, Mary Doreen. Remember that I've laid in some of those frozen TV dinners to start you off tonight."

"Sure, Mom," Dodo replies, doodling on her paper napkin. "You know, I've got an idea for a peach of a painting, just as soon as I'm on my feet again."

It's a frieze of dancing children in a meadow of flowers and birds, and it goes on the walls of the playroom of the YWCA's nursery. Dodo goes there to paint at night after Mike has had his dinner and the babies are asleep. But the happy picture is at odds with her blue mood. And after her fourth child is born, the morning comes when Dodo can't or won't get out of bed, and the ambulance comes once more to whisk her away.

"Fairfield Hills is lovely," Mrs. Dougherty tells Betty and Zora, referring to the state psychiatric hospital in Newtown. "All the buildings are made of red brick with white columns, surrounded by a lovely green lawn. Dodo says the place is like a college campus. And she is learning in therapy to paint in water colors."

This time, when Dodo comes home, she brings her medication with her. Miltown is the wonder drug that makes her feel so much better.

"Do you know, Betty, that even Milton Berle takes it? And if Uncle Miltie says it's okay, it must be."

Dodo describes the long, narrow tunnels that connect all the buildings at Fairfield Hills.

"Imagine it, Betty. All the doctors and nurses are dressed in white uniforms. And the patients are in their bathrobes. Summer and winter, day and night, back and forth they go, in and out of the buildings, connected by those tunnels underground. You'd never imagine they were there beneath the lawns and sidewalks when you go to see the place. I went through the tunnels myself, on the way to shock therapy."

Seeing the expression on Betty's face, Dodo explains that shock is not as bad as she might think.

"You get retrograde amnesia from the electroconvulsive shock, and so you really don't remember the treatment. All you know is that you're feeling better."

All the buildings at Fairfield Hills are named for Connecticut cities and towns. Dodo's dorm was called Litchfield.

"Of course, no one wanted to transfer to Yale at this campus," she laughs, explaining that Yale at Fairfield Hills is the name of the building that houses morgue. It is plain to Betty that Dodo has enjoyed her stay there.

Dodo becomes animated as she tells that she was invited to paint a mural in the main tunnel.

"I did a big painting of the whole campus. I drew all sixteen of the red brick buildings clustered under autumn colored trees. My doctor gave me a postcard picture to work from. It came out really nice. Maybe you could go there and see it for yourself," she adds.

"It was as if she was describing a resort instead of a hospital!" Betty tells her husband that night.

On the advice of Father Reilly, the Kajak family begins going to Sunday Mass as a family. The children line up on the front porch holding hands for the walk to Saint Margaret's, all except baby Donald, who rides wide-eyed in his carriage. The little boys look, as Betty's husband describes it, like steps of stairs. Rob hums a song he knows with lyrics about "building a stairway to the stars." He begins to sing it, dancing around the kitchen while Betty tells him there is nothing remotely funny about four children so close together in age.

"But Dodo is taking happy pills now," he replies. "Things may be tough, but now she's the last one to know it."

"Dodo has asked me to be her mother's helper this summer," Betts tells them over supper. "Baby five is on the way, and her doctor says there's a good chance it will turn out to be twins. Another pair of hands is what Dodo says she needs."

"I'd say she has too many hands at work over there as it is," says Zora, who has come for a visit and been treated to the latest neighborhood gossip.

Dodo's next-door neighbor Mrs. Gemmalino has happened to glance into the Kajak's bathroom window one night last week and witnessed them "going at it like dogs, from behind." Mrs. Gemmalino is glad to describe to Betty how shocked she was, but that of course it was their own fault for not pulling down the shade.

"He had her up against the bathroom sink. What an animal," she concluded.

"You know, Betts, I think it's better for you to stay at home. I can use your help myself," Betty says. What she means is that Dodo's life has gone so far downhill that the young woman with art talent is no longer a suitable role model.

May is the month Catholics celebrate the Blessed Virgin Mary, and Betts has been asked by her teacher, Mother Saint John of Mercy, to paint a basket of spring flowers to cut out and pin to the classroom bulletin board. Betts goes across the street to ask if she can borrow Dodo's paints.

"Oh, honey. They all dried out long ago. I threw them away in the trash. But while you're here, come and look at what Mike and I just bought." Three sets of bunk beds are pushed against the walls of the old nursery nearly obscuring the characters in the Mother Goose mural.

"Wasn't it lucky that I had that rainy day fund from when I used to paint?"

Betts feels sad to see the mural hidden. She can just make out the head of the white cat, a slice of the smiling moon. It feels to her as if she's lost a friend.

"We'll get you your own paints," Betts's mother tells her. "We'll go downtown to Goldsmith's after school."

"I'll need brushes too, Mom. Dodo said she can't think where hers went, it's been so long since she's seen them."

When the basket of flowers is completed in a rainbow of colors with carefully drawn green leaves, Betts takes her artwork to show Dodo. Mike is mowing the lawn without his shirt, something Betts's mother frowns on as an unsuitable display of epidermis. The boys are running wild, playing Indians with a makeshift bow. Their arrows, on close inspection, prove to be Dodo's lost paintbrushes.

Betts waits for Dodo to say something about it, to tell the boys that her brushes are off-limits because she needs them for herself. But she sees that it is as unlikely to happen as a cow jumping over the moon.

"Oh, let them have them," says Dodo. "None of that's important any more."

FATHER DOOLEY'S COTTAGE

July in the inner city is not for the faint of heart. Most mornings, it was even hotter when I woke up than it had been the night before when I'd spread out in my cotton nightgown on my bottom sheet to sleep, hoping for a breeze that never came. The organdy tiebacks on my windows hung motionless.

But this particular July was different because we were going to Father Dooley's cottage for a week's vacation. And we were going there today.

My family had never gone on a vacation before, and I was eleven. When my parents told me about the cottage, I was flabbergasted. My imagination was a vivid one, but I'd never imagined a priest with a beach cottage all his own. An even bigger surprise was the fact that we owned suitcases. When Dad produced an assortment of luggage from our attic, it was as entertaining as the TV magician who'd produced a dove from his black top hat. Dad handed the bags down through the opening in the upstairs hall ceiling to my grandfather, who steadied the ladder for his climb.

I chose the blue leather suitcase with little brass locks for my own. I packed my flowered bathing suit with its modest, pleated skirt, a dress for Sunday Mass, and the usual shorts and tops, but I left room for books. My mother said that I ate books. Although I knew from English class that Mom's words were a metaphor, in a way it was true: all the stories that I had devoured were now inside me, in my brain.

Before we got into the car, Dad checked all the rooms in our house. He pulled the window shades down to their sills, made sure the faucets weren't dripping, locked the front and back and cellar doors, and we were on our way.

"Good-bye, house. Good-bye, street. Good-bye, alley cats," called Molly, waving from the rear window of our car. Even though she was only four, my sister clearly understood how big an event this vacation trip was. Dad's parents were going too, and our two cars formed a caravan all the way to Rhode Island. I'd fallen asleep around Middletown and I came awake to the smell of salty air through the open windows. I could see a flash of ocean and a flock of sea gulls touching down on sand.

"This is it, kids. Misquamicut, Rhode Island," Dad announced.

"I'm hungry," said Molly from her side of the backseat. Mom handed her a cookie.

"Can we go there?" she asked as we passed an amusement park with a big Ferris wheel.

"What about that place? Can we go there too?" she added as Dad's car zoomed by a beach shack store called Cisco's, its front nearly obscured by multicolored plastic water wings, rubber rafts, and every kind of water toy known to beach going revelers in 1956.

"We'll see," Dad replied.

Our road ran parallel to the beach, and I studied the bathers carefully, knowing that soon we'd be among them. The road was black topped, and I could smell the tar warming in the noon day sun. We turned up a narrow lane, and Molly and I began to guess at which cottage would be ours. When I saw the white bungalow with green shutters, I fell in love.

"Hit the deck, kids," said Dad as he began to unload the car. Out came pillows, sheets, towels, cardboard cartons of groceries, and our Monopoly game, packed by Grandma as insurance against a possible rainy day. Molly and I circled the house, not wanting to miss a thing. The cottage's thick green lawn felt like carpet beneath our new sneakers. We poked into the outdoor shower and changing room attached to the white garage, then went inside.

"A fireplace!" said Molly. "And it's made of little round stones like the ones you find on a beach."

"The two downstairs bedrooms are for grown-ups," said Grandma, appearing from the pantry. "You girls will sleep upstairs."

Our vacation bedroom was the whole second floor of the house, with a built-in bureau in each of its gables. Twin beds stood beneath the sloping roof, with double windows at each end. The entire room, walls and ceiling too, was paneled in golden pine that glowed in the bright afternoon sunlight. There was even a little rainbow on one corner of the floor where a sunbeam caught the light reflected in the bedroom's mirror.

"Our room is the color of honey," said Molly. "I'm going to pretend we are bees in a hive."

I unpacked my books on the night table between our beds, but I had the feeling I would not be reading them. The breeze through the windows we'd opened was telling me to go outside.

"Beach time, girls," called Mom. Dad gathered up our big red umbrella and the scratchy woolen blanket marked US Navy. It was a hot walk in the afternoon sun, but worth it when we reached the ocean.

"It's so big," said Molly as she ran toward it with her pail and shovel. But what I noticed most about it was its sound. The roar of the waves as they came in, broke, and receded was so alive it was like the voice of a friendly lion. We all put on our sunglasses, and Grandma broke out the Coppertone.

"You look like you should be in the movies," Grandpa told Molly, pointing to her sunglasses with their red frames in the shapes of stars. My frames were plain white plastic, but their tinted lenses gave everything I saw a rosy glow. Dad set up the umbrella while Grandpa spread the blanket. Molly got busy in the sand, but I climbed a dune to look around. When I reached the top, I was surprised to find myself looking down into the foundation of a house.

"The house that was there was swept out to sea in the Hurricane of 1938," said an old man seated in the dune with his sketch pad. Just beyond the foundation was a small salt pond, and on it were two swans. They were the biggest ones I'd ever seen, and whiter than a new box of chalk. I'd learned a poem in school about swans, though I could only recall the first few lines:

Stately swan so proud and white
Glistening in the morning light

Its author, Evaleen Stein, had gone on for a couple of verses about fairy lands and fables and magic. At the time, I'd thought it silly, but now I wished I could remember more of it.

"I like to draw them," the artist confided. "Swans are symbols of love, you know."

Unlike Waterbury, July in Misquamicut is cooled by a steady ocean breeze. Even the sun seemed kinder, glinting off the endless pale sand and the wild pink roses that grew around the pond where the swans idled. The sky was a big blue bowl turned upside down. I felt overwhelmed with my good fortune.

"I love it here," I told my mother as she passed around the sandwiches.

"Why not," she answered. "You were conceived in Rhode Island during the war when your father was stationed in Newport."

This was news to me. I guessed that Mom had been so relaxed by the combination of sun, sea, and sky that she'd unbent enough just this once to share information about a topic known in our house as the birds and the bees. I couldn't think of anything to say back, so I simply looked thoughtful and buried my feet in the sand.

"Come down where the sand is wet," Molly called. "I'm building a castle."

Molly's castle was shaped with help from her upended bucket and decorated with pebbles. I mounded up some sand and patted it into a rectangle with dormers.

"That's not our house you're making," Dad said. "It looks like Father Dooley's."

"If you girls want to see some real castles," he continued, "I'll take you to Watch Hill tomorrow. You can see how rich people spend their summer vacation."

At breakfast next morning, Mom was wearing a dress.

"Put your Sunday clothes on, girls," she said. "You'll want to look like little ladies when we go to Watch Hill." All six of us climbed into Grandpa's Chevy for the ride and rolled into town past the biggest hotel I'd ever seen. Its massive wooden sides were painted pale yellow. Ocean House was the name on its sign above the white columned portico. A doorman in livery stood beneath the hotel's porte cochere helping guests out of their cars.

"We'll skip the Ocean House today," Dad joked. "I left my tuxedo at home."

We parked on Bay Street and walked along narrow sidewalks, peering into the shop windows at clothes and hats and sandals. The window displays had backdrops of golf clubs and croquet sets and photos of yachts like the ones on our right, tied up to the Watch Hill dock. All of the big boats were white, with shiny chrome trim. One even had a real captain on board, with gold braid on the shoulders of his shirt.

"This place is too rich for my blood," said Grandpa. "I'll be over there on a bench when you're ready."

The bench he'd selected was next to the statue of an Indian who was crouching on one knee. He was nearly naked except for a breech cloth, and his headband had only two feathers, one of them crooked. Our own Waterbury Indian, Chief Two Moon, dressed in a hand beaded leather suit and a big war bonnet full of feathers, so I was surprised to learn that this Indian, identified by a bronze plaque as Ninigret, had been a chief as well. Ninigret's statue had been sculpted with a big open mouthed fish on each side of him beneath his down turned palms. They seemed to be his pets, a finny version of lap dogs, I guessed.

"I'll be here keeping an eye on this Indian," Grandpa told us. But Molly coaxed him to walk with her to the end of Bay Street.

"I see a merry-go-round down there," she coaxed, tugging at his hand.

"Ah, yes, the flying horses," replied a lady walking her white poodle. She seemed eager to get in on our conversation.

"Did you know that those wooden horses have real horsehair manes and tails and agate eyes? People say this is the oldest carousel in the USA," she continued.

"I hope they have a palomino like Roy Rogers's horse, Trigger," Molly exclaimed. "I wish I'd brought my cowboy hat."

"If you catch the brass ring you will get a free ride, little girl," the lady called after them.

"There is no free ride," Grandpa replied. But the lady smiled at him as if she hadn't heard.

Mom and Grandma were choosing postcards from a rack on the sidewalk, so I ducked into a store filled with books. The books were old and stacked any old way on shelves and tables. The place had a musty smell that reminded me of the velvet confessional curtain at Saint Margaret's Church back home. There were postcards here too, dog-eared and yellowed. The store's musty smell made me lightheaded, but the old books were so interesting that I had to look around. Down in back, I found a little one about the size of my *Saint Joseph Sunday Missal.* The book's cover was white with a sheaf of lilies embossed in gold. The ends of the pages were gold, too. "Gold Dust" was the book's title, and when I looked inside I saw that there were 366 thoughts, one for every day of the year plus leap year.

"How much is this book?" I asked. It seemed that I was meant to find it, and it was too beautiful to leave behind.

"For you, young lady, a quarter," the store owner replied. "It's refreshing to see a girl in a dress."

I caught up with my mother and grandmother a few stores down. They were looking at a window display with a pocketbook at its center. It was a white straw basket with a golden clasp and a pink ribbon around it in the latest fashion color, known as shocking pink. The lid of the basket was topped with a pink felt square like a tablecloth. On top of it, four little toy white lady mice in flowered hats were playing Bridge. The mice had martini glasses beside their hands of cards and tiny shell ashtrays with little pretend cigarettes in them.

"Can you beat it?" said Mom. "Forty dollars for that!"

"Now that's a pocketbook that you will never find in Waterbury," Grandma replied. "Not even in Howland-Hughes."

I saw at once that the purse was the height of sophistication. I pictured myself carrying it to Mass on Sunday. But its cost was nearly a week's worth of groceries at the A&P on Cooke Street. And my mother's reaction to the frivolous, card-playing lady mice told me it would be best not to admit how much I admired it.

Dad and Grandpa were waiting for us at the carousel.

"I was too little to catch the brass ring," Molly told us. "But Grandpa bought me another ride anyway."

We lingered in front of a souvenir shop's window. And that was where I saw the china swans. There was a big one like a mother swan, with a little matching cygnet beside her. The swans were a set and small enough to fit in the palm of my hand.

"Go ahead, go in and get them," said Grandpa, handing me a dollar bill. I held them all the way back to the cottage.

Upstairs in our room I began to read *Gold Dust*. Every single day's thought was a happy one. The topics were things like mothers and pets and love. And the thought for this day, the very day on which I'd bought the book, read, "Where your treasure is, there will be your heart." I wondered if it was a secret message meant just for me.

I'd heard that if you left something behind you in a place you loved, it could work as a charm to guarantee you'd return again. I thought about what I could leave in Misquamicut. I knew that it would have to be something with a special meaning to me. My clothes didn't count, and I could hardly leave a library book behind. My new china swans sat on the bedside table, shining in the light from my lamp. I hated to separate them, but the more I thought about it, the surer I became that one of my swans would be the talisman that did the trick.

Next morning when we went to the beach I took the big swan along. I tucked her into the sand by a corner of the lost house's foundation right where she could see the swan pond. I drew a map of where I'd left her, with an X that marked the spot. When we went back to the cottage, I hid the map in a crack in the knotty pine paneling behind my bed.

The rest of the week was sunny. We spent every day at the beach, so I was able to check and see how my swan was doing. And at night after supper, we all sat out on the cottage's back lawn in Father Dooley's Adirondack chairs and watched the stars. Molly had brought along some sparklers left over from Fourth of July, and we set them out in the lawn and lit them.

"Star light, star bright," she began, wishing on a star. "You make one too, Betts."

My wish was that we could stay in the cottage forever. Since that seemed unlikely, I added a wish that I could live there myself when I grew up.

On our last day of vacation, we stayed late at the beach watching the waves roll in.

"Good-bye," Molly called to the ocean as we drove away.

It was as hot in Waterbury when we returned as it had been the day we left. When I went inside our house, everything inside it was exactly the same there too.

"It's good to be home," Grandma told Mom. And in a way, it was. I was glad to see my room and my dolls and my own bed again. It was my world. But since Father Dooley's cottage, I'd seen for myself that the world was a whole lot bigger.

I reached into my pocket and set the little china swan on my bedside table.

"Don't worry," I told it. "Your mom is fine. And we'll be back there again before you know it."

"Did you kids have fun?" asked Dad at supper.

"Yes!" Molly and I answered in unison, making our parents laugh.

When I got into my bed that night, I picked up the little swan and held him to my ear as if he was the chambered seashell Dad had found on the beach.

"Put it to your ear. You'll hear the ocean," he'd told me.

"Good night. Sleep tight," I whispered in the dark.

As I began to fall asleep, I thought about my big china swan back in Misquamicut, nestled in the warm sand, watching the real swans swim. It was a pretty thought, and it stayed with me long after I had turned out my light.

YANKEE DOODLE DANDY

Zora is fanning herself with the front section of the *Waterbury Republican*, looking out her kitchen window at the morning sky. The shades are drawn in the rest of the house. Today will be a scorcher, and it's only mid-May. There's an open book in front of her on the kitchen table.

"Three branches of government," she murmurs. "Executive. Legislative. Judicial."

Zora is studying to become a citizen of the United States of America. Donal, her husband, became one back in the 1930s when they came to Waterbury from Ireland.

Zora's path has been a different one. She is going to be naturalized. And her ceremony is just around the corner, in the month of June. For Americans, June is school graduation month. And so June seems to Zora an entirely appropriate time for the ceremony.

"I am like a graduate myself," she murmurs, "with all this testing." She has been examined on her skills in reading and writing, and her fingerprints have been taken and sent off with an application her daughter Betty filled out on her black Royal typewriter.

The civics test is the last of the business, and then Zora will be sent her ceremony date through the US mail.

"President Dwight David Eisenhower," she says as she gets up to put on her hat. Surely everyone knows the answer to that question, she thinks. Zora picks up her patent leather purse and puts on her white gloves. She is going to Betty's today, and it is almost time to catch the bus at its Hamilton Avenue stop.

Inside Woolworth's where she waits with her transfer for the Overlook bus, Zora selects a cellophane packet of three white shells that when dropped into water will open into paper flower bouquets. She's bought them before, she knows her granddaughter will like them. As she passes the jewelry counter on her way out, her attention is caught by a display of rhinestone pins on little cardboard backs. "Old Glory," it says in royal blue script at the tops of the cards above the red, white, and blue flags.

"Why not?" she thinks, and hands the saleswoman fifty-nine cents in exchange for her purchase which is slipped into a small brown paper bag.

At one o'clock, she and Betty and Betty's mother-in-law, Cora, go back downtown to Betts's school for the May procession. All the girls in grades one through eight march through the garden and circle the outdoor statue of the Blessed Virgin Mary, praying the Joyful Mysteries out loud on their rosaries. The life-sized white statue is set high on a pedestal in the walled garden behind the brick mansion turned Catholic girls' school. An eighth-grade girl in her mother's wedding dress crowns the statue with a wreath of spring flowers and the aid of a step stool while the girls sing:

O Mary, we crown thee with blossoms today!
Queen of the angels! Queen of the May!

Zora watches, holding her own mother-of-pearl rosary. She fingers the Child of Mary holy medal she received when she was Betts's age, from the nuns at her school in Killarney. Zora likes the continuity of the May ceremony honoring Mary, a new generation of little girls doing the same things she once did, albeit on the other side of the Atlantic Ocean and in a modern world.

That night at supper, they talk about their day and Zora's studies. She and Betts discover that her Civics book and Betts's fourth grade history text cover much of the same material.

"Who was the first president of the United States?"

"George Washington!" They laugh, then move on to harder questions.

"What is the name of the first ten amendments of the Constitution?"

"The Bill of Rights."

Zora remembers the present she bought that morning and takes it from her purse.

"Here. Put these things in water, and we'll watch them grow."

Betts gets a glass of water, and they wait for the shells to open. The paper flowers in this batch are white and orange, with green streamers that look like vines.

"Thank you, Grandma," says Betts, kissing Zora's cheek. No one remarks that the flowers are in the colors of the Irish flag, or that this could be an omen.

"Nice photo, Mom," Betty tells her, referring to the picture taken for her citizenship application.

"You ought to get your passport while you're at it," Cora says. "You might like to go back to Ireland some time."

"Why not, Mom? Why not go this summer? You'll be a genuine American by then, so they can't keep you over there," jokes Rob.

"We'll see," says Zora, continuing to eat her meat and potatoes. Donal looks across the table at her. His expression looks worried. Perhaps he is afraid she will indeed go and not come back. Zora knows there is no chance of that happening. She is firmly rooted here in the US of A, as her citizenship classmate Mr. Mancini calls it. But it won't hurt Donal to worry a bit, she thinks.

What would it be like to return now to the land of memories, with a trunk full of new clothes, a new summer hat, photos of her grandchildren? I'd be a regular Scheherazade, she thinks, regaling her sister with tales of copious amounts of running hot water, and busses at all hours to everywhere, and department stores. I'd return like a queen, she thinks, and smiles.

"I'd go by boat, of course," she says.

The family looks up, surprised that she'd really consider it. Then Betty says, "I'll pick up a passport application for you at the post office when I go for stamps."

"But first things first," Zora tells her. "I've still the books to hit for that exam."

Zora has bought a new dress for the ceremony, to reward herself for passing the test with what the examiner has called flying colors. It's navy blue with a wide white grosgrain collar. The saleswoman at Howland-Hughes has assured her it is an unbeatable combination, suitably dignified, yet stylish.

Donal drops her off at the brick and marble Grand Street palace called Waterbury City Hall. The fountain's spray is glistening in the late afternoon sun. She takes her place in the lineup in the chambers in between Mr. Mancini and Mrs. Grebowki. Mayor Snyder is on hand in a gray suit next to the judge. The candidates take the oath of allegiance together:

> I hereby declare, on oath, that I absolutely and entirely
> Renounce and abjure all allegiance and fidelity to any
> Foreign prince, potentate, state or sovereignty of whom
> Or which I have heretofore been a subject or citizen,
> That I will support and defend the Constitution and laws
> Of the United States of America against all her enemies,
> Foreign and domestic.

There's more, of course, ending with the phrase "So help me God."

A clerk passes out welcome packets with a letter from the president of the United States, Dwight David Eisenhower, a detail Zora notes with satisfaction. There is a *Citizen's Almanac,* as well, and a pocket-sized Declaration of Independence. The packet includes a copy of the Constitution and a voter's guide. There's even a passport application, but she has already gotten hers, filled it out, and sent it on its way to the powers that be.

The newly minted citizens mill around the hall, smiling and shaking each other's hands.

"Good luck," calls Mr. Mancini as he joins his family.

Donal's car is waiting outside at the curb. You wouldn't think that a few official words would make a palpable difference in her perspective, but they have. Zora exits City Hall with a new sense of ownership.

"My city," she tells herself. "My country. My flag." She smiles with satisfaction. They drive up Willow Street to Betty's for cake and coffee. In fact, she feels elated. She feels that she ought to be waving to the passersby, telling them her news.

"I see you've a new brooch," says Donal, referring to her glittering rhinestone flag. It's pinned above her silver Tara brooch, a little to the left.

"I have indeed," Zora replies. "Put that in your pipe and smoke it."

Fourth of July rolls around, a day so hot that the cats have taken refuge beneath the porch rather than their usual perches on the car hoods in the sun. At Betty's house, the front and back lawns are freshly mowed, the children's wading pool filled with cold water. The charcoal grill is set up on its tripod legs, and hot dogs and hamburger from Dave's Superette are ready in the refrigerator.

"We're off to the parade," Donal says, "and as usual, it will be a jim-dandy one." They choose a location on the Green to watch the marchers so that the women can sit on the benches. Boy Scouts and baton twirlers, beauty queens and local dignitaries in convertible cars, the Knights of Columbus and the Mattatuck Drum Corps thundering out their regimental tunes all pass by, interspersed with balloon sellers and ice cream vendors. An enormous American flag is carried past them, billowing out in the breeze. It is followed by a band playing "The Stars and Stripes Forever." Pretty soon, the sky is dotted with tiny colored circles of balloons that have escaped from their little owners' hands. There is no balloon for Betts this year, she has decided that she is too big now for them. Her little sister Molly has followed suit, choosing instead a paper bird on a long stick.

"This will drive our cats crazy when I twirl it," she laughs.

When they get home, Rob sets the canvas deck chairs out on the back lawn by the lilac tree. The grandmothers put their feet in the wading pool. Its wavy blue lines seem to ripple in the last of the sun's rays.

"Anyone for going to the fireworks?" asks Rob. They are set off each Fourth at the Municipal Stadium when it is finally dark.

"I've had enough excitement for one day," Betty answers. The others nod assent.

"My dogs are barking," says Donal, with a reference to his feet that never fails to draw a laugh. Around them, the crowded neighborhood comes to life with its own firecrackers, and there is even an occasional red glare from rockets set off above them on Ridgewood Street. Rob breaks out the sparklers and lights one for each of his girls, who trail them in loops and circles until the box is emptied.

"It was a grand day entirely, and a beautiful birthday party for the USA," says Zora, fingering her flag pin as if it might magically light up into its own display of lights.

"Ah, you're a regular Yankee Doodle Dandy now," Donal tells her. Though he says it as a joke, he is proud of his wife, he just can't or won't say so.

Zora is silent, so he adds, "Sure it's a fine thing to be. In fact, aren't we all Yankee Doodle Dandies?"

Donal is worried that his wife is miffed, that he may have offended her with his funny remark. But he is mistaken. Zora's thoughts are a thousand miles away, though not as far away as Ireland. What she is thinking about is those shells she bought for Betts a while ago, and how they opened into flowers. It seems to her that she has blossomed too, set down here in Waterbury, Connecticut.

You would never have imagined all this, she thinks, looking back to the day she and Donal first met. She feels that she is floating in the warm darkness of the backyard. Her heart is open wide. In the distance, they can hear the rocket finale at the Municipal Stadium. The fireworks are signaling the end of the Fourth of July, but for Zora, the celebration has just begun.

GOING PLACES

The white convertible flashed up and down Willow Street all summer, its red upholstery gleaming in the sun. The woman next to the driver wore a silky head scarf around her hair, tied beneath her chin like Marilyn Monroe. The driver's arm hung casually out his open car window holding a cigarette. And a girl my age with brown braids sat squarely in the middle of its wide backseat.

At the end of the summer, the girl with brown braids walked past my house with her grandmother while I was on the front lawn.

"Hello," I said. And that was my password into the world of the McMahons.

Dana, my new friend, lived in the Bernard Apartments, a yellow brick fortress at the corner of our block. I took my first ride in an elevator there, to their third-floor apartment at the end of a long dark hall.

The L-shaped apartment had two doors, the kitchen one with a frosted-glass windowpane and the living room door with an assertive doorbell set to one side of the brass plate meant to hold a name card. The living room had a wide, mysterious closet in its long wall. Dana's mother opened it to show me a brown metal bed that folded down when she pulled on it. She called it a Murphy bed and explained that it was where she and Mr. McMahon slept at night.

Dana had the apartment's single bedroom, painted in a color Dana's mother called Mamie Eisenhower Pink. In one corner stood a pink changing screen just like ones I'd seen in movies. From Dana's bedroom's window, I could see my house's front walk. But once I was in their apartment, my home seemed light years away.

Each morning, the McMahons drove off to work, leaving Dana with her grandmother, Mrs. Riley. Because I was so curious about apartment life Mrs. Riley took us to the top floor to visit her studio apartment. I was captivated by its teeny kitchenette behind French doors, its Murphy bed, which by now I believed was standard for all apartment living, and its tiny black and white-tiled bath.

"Here's where I hang my hat, gals," Mrs. Riley said, lighting a Lucky Strike with her monogrammed lighter. "But I do my living below in Dana's place." Mrs. Riley's clothes were completely unlike anything your average Willow Street housewife would wear. The crinolines beneath her calf-length pink-and-black-checked circle skirt swished as she walked around the room.

"Christian Dior's new look,'" she explained, as if she believed I knew the ins and outs of the French fashion.

"Of course, *Vogue* is reporting a newer look on the horizon," she mused. "But this look is mine." To compliment her look, Mrs. Riley rolled her shoulder length white hair up each morning into a tidy cylinder she called a French twist.

"Now my daughter Rhoda's look is up to the minute," Mrs. Riley continued. "She's a career gal, and Mac is a go-getter. With our arrangement, they can come and go as they please. Of course, Dana and I have our own fun too," she added, reapplying her lipstick. She was so good at it that she could put it on without using a mirror.

The McMahons' apartment was lined with shelves of best sellers delivered each month from Book of the Month Club. Their living room coffee table was stacked with magazines: *Vogue, Redbook, Good Housekeeping, Photoplay.* I was not surprised that after I'd arrived and said hello, Mrs. Riley would wave us on our way while she settled in with what she called her book du jour. For an Irish lady, Mrs. Riley sure knew a lot of French.

The McMahons' library was as much a draw for me as my friend Dana, and I began to come early so I could read too. The glossy magazines with their color-photo layouts introduced me to a parallel universe where everything was shiny and new. The photos were as intriguing to me as illustrations from fairy tales. I marveled at long, low ranch houses with breezeways and barbeque pits, pastel-colored kitchen appliances, tiny hot dogs stuck into pineapples with toothpicks to be served at parties, and swimming pools with turquoise water and their own little cabanas. And I saw right away that the photos of dresses and shoes in the latest styles were exactly like the ones that Rhoda McMahon wore each day to work.

If I'd had to put the difference between Dana's world and mine into words based on the recipes I'd read in *McCall's*, I'd have said that our house was meatloaf and potatoes. But the McMahons' was chicken a la king.

"Come to dinner Friday. It's Dana's birthday," said her mother. "I'll telephone your mom with the invite."

When Rhoda McMahon opened the door in her shimmery green taffeta party dress, I was glad my mother had told me to wear my own best duds.

"Come on in, moonbeam," she said, gesturing with the hand that held her drink. Her long oval fingernails were painted red, just like the model I'd seen in a Hazel Bishop makeup ad in *Redbook*. Behind her in the hall, Mr. McMahon was mixing drinks from the brass and glass teacart they had set up as a bar.

"How about a highball, Daisy?" he called to Mrs. Riley in the kitchen.

I could never have imagined that Dana's parents would go to so much trouble for two little girls. We dined by candlelight on a card table set up in the living room. There was a pink rose in a china bud vase, and our napkins matched the pink linen cloth. Dana's father served us with a dish towel over one arm.

"I'm just like a waiter at Diorio's Restaurant," he joked. Dana and I could hear the grown-ups laughing in the kitchen as we ate our chicken and sipped our Shirley Temples. It was obvious that cocktail hour at the McMahons' was a lot of fun.

"How was the party?" my mother asked me when I got home.

My question to her, asked at nearly the same moment, was "Why don't you and Daddy have a cocktail hour?"

Mom was sitting in our kitchen's platform rocker, reading the newspaper. She'd kicked off her shoes and put her feet up on the little red hassock. Our radio was set to WATR, and it was playing the very same song I'd just listened to on the McMahons' record player, a song about three coins in a fountain, searching for happiness. It amazed me that the same song could sound either entirely possible or completely unreal depending on where you were when you heard it.

"Molly is awake. She's waiting up for you," Mom said. Every night, I tucked my sister in with a song I'd made up about a sleepy kitten. Molly was crazy about cats, and I was the only one besides Molly who knew it, so I'd become an indispensable part of my two-year-old sister's bedtime routine. I always followed my song with a story I made up as I went along. Even though I was nine, I enjoyed it all as much as Molly did.

I noticed that in the lamplight, my mother's hair was the same shade of auburn as Rhoda McMahon's.

"You'd look pretty in a green dress," I told her.

My mother sighed.

"Honey, your Dad wants me home while you kids are little. It wouldn't make sense for me to dress up like Dana's mother just to do housework. And as for cocktails, we never drink unless there's a special occasion." Turning off the radio, she added, "I'm glad you had fun. It sounded really glamorous."

I remembered the day we'd first spied the McMahons in their car and how my mother had said they were going places. Since Molly's arrival, my mother had stuck close to home. I could tell she missed working. Mom was even prettier than Rhoda McMahon, and I wondered if she wished she could go out every day in heels and makeup, in Grandma's words, "dressed to kill."

The McMahons' glamorous lifestyle extended beyond apartment living and work. It included weekends, too. Dana's dad was a Knight of Columbus and marched in parades wearing a flowing black cape with a purple satin lining and a big hat with a feathered plume. I'd gone with them to the Knights' clubhouse on Mitchell Avenue once, after a minstrel show at Wilby High's auditorium. The big, spooky Victorian mansion was shabby, but its shabbiness seemed to highlight the glittery sophisticated crowd, whose last names, I noticed, were mostly Irish.

The women in my family had their glamorous moments, of course, though not often enough for my taste. Sunday Mass was our family's main occasion for style. Depending on the season, it meant Grandma's stone marten fur piece and handbag with petit point flowers or Mom's new winter coat with its sparkly topaz-colored jeweled buttons. But most of the time these things stayed put in drawers or closets, which seemed to me inexplicable.

"We save them for good in case we need to go someplace," said Grandma, which seemed to me to be no real answer at all.

I continued my study of the McMahons' magazines and began to pick up tips. I learned what to say in a "bread and butter note" of thanks, handy for the strange gifts my uncle's wife bought for my birthday and for Christmas, to help me sound grateful. I vowed never to wear white shoes before Memorial Day or after Labor Day, because to do so was a fashion faux pas. And I memorized the diagram of the proper way to set a table. From that day on, I arranged the knives and spoons on the right of the plate and the fork on its left alongside a precisely folded triangular paper napkin when I set the kitchen table for our supper, and made sure the flower design in the center of our plates was placed right side up.

On days when Dana and I left the apartment, shooed out by Mrs. Riley to get fresh air, we walked along Hillside Avenue. We liked to see the mansions. Although they were a bit worse for wear in 1954, to us they were magical. We played a game of choosing which one would someday be ours. Once we'd peered into the windows of a house on Kellogg Street and seen gilded ballroom chairs set up around a grand piano. The house's uniformed maid had suddenly appeared, and we'd scattered, hearts pounding over our daring.

Mrs. Riley had made friends with the housekeeper of a shingled Newport-style house on the Hillside, and Bessie sometimes invited us in to a kitchen bigger than the whole first floor of my house. When she offered us cookies, I ate carefully, one hand cupped in my lap as *McCall's* advised. One day, Bessie offered to show us through the mansion's downstairs rooms, its double parlors with doors that could disappear into the walls, its wide, shadowy hall with its massive staircase, and its dining room with red geraniums in the sunny south facing window beyond a table with twenty chairs.

"Where are the people who live here?" I whispered.

"Oh, they're always going places," the housekeeper told us. "They won't be back till spring."

On our way home, Dana and I linked arms. "Let's sing," she said, as we skipped along, careful not to step on cracks and break our mothers' backs.

"Mr. Sandman," she began. "Bring me a dream."

"What would your dream be?" I asked her.

"A puppy," she said. "How about you?"

I thought about the mansion we'd just visited, Rhoda McMahon's fabulous clothes, the pictures in all those magazines. None of it was anything like my own life on Willow Street. I saw that making a wish would change things if it came true. To make a wish required a lot of thought.

"I don't know," I answered. And that was the absolute truth.

Saturday came, and Dana's parents dressed for their regular night out on the town. Mrs. McMahon was changing behind the pink screen in Dana's bedroom. We sat on the bed to help her decide what to wear. She emerged in a blue silk dress with a deep V-neckline and a string of pearls. She anointed herself with Tigress perfume from the bottle with a furry little tiger-striped cap and held up her bangle bracelets for us to see.

"Too much, ladies?" she asked.

"No!" we shouted in unison. How could anything so wonderful be too much?

Though September had begun, the weather was still hot. A faint sheen of perspiration gave Mrs. McMahon a glow as she leaned down to kiss us good-night. Her perfume smelled musky and mysterious. I marveled that any woman could walk into a store and buy whatever perfume she wanted, regardless of her lifestyle.

Did the saleswoman in the rhinestone studded, cat's eye glasses at Worth's perfume counter on Bank Street suspect, as she rang up each purchase and tucked it into one of the store's signature pink-and-gray-striped bags with its logo written diagonally in quarter-inch high pink script that not every bottle of magical scent would be put to its highest use?

My mother had a box of Elizabeth Arden Blue Grass on her mahogany dresser. Its pale aqua gold-rimmed rectangular box was still in its cellophane wrap, reflected in the mirror. On the front of the box, a golden horse jumped through a wreath of golden flowers. Although this particular bottle had found its way to our house via downtown Waterbury, Connecticut, its label boasted that the *parfum* inside was most commonly found in the glamour cities of London, Paris, and New York.

The perfume bottle seemed to hint that my mother might entertain thoughts of a different life as she swept the porch or bent over the soapstone tubs in our cellar. There was no hint of Blue Grass there, only soap and steam.

"Dana tells me that your father is an artist," Rhoda McMahon began. I knew she was referring to the murals on our cellar walls, painted by Dad after supper, for fun. He'd told me I could choose my favorite cartoon characters, and so Snow White danced with the Seven Dwarfs above Dad's workbench while Bugs Bunny and Elmer Fudd watched over Mom as she fed the wash through the wringer of her machine.

"Do you think if I ask him, he would do a mural for us on our living room wall? We're throwing a cocktail party. It would be the perfect touch."

Dad agreed and worked up a design from one of their *New Yorker* magazines. Dad drew a big white circle on their green wall, and in it he sketched a snooty man in a top hat and monocle, a martini glass, and a pair of folded white gloves. He worked on it at night after work for almost a week. And when he was done, the McMahons invited him and my mother to their party.

My mother wore her red flowered dress and patent leather heels and her Monet charm bracelet with the little gold metal charms you could hook yourself on one at a time as you bought them. She opened her new box of Blue Grass and sprayed some on behind her ears. It smelled like carnations on a breezy summer day. Mom paused a moment, holding the golden atomizer's ball, then spritzed some on me too.

"Pretty nice, isn't it?" she said as she applied her lipstick. In *Vogue*, I'd learned that the way a woman wore her lipstick down in its tube was a clue to her personality. Rhoda McMahon wore hers evenly, maintaining its perfect shape right down to the very last bit. *Vogue* said that this meant she was cool and collected. My mother's lipstick, on the other hand, quickly became a blunted tip, indicating, according to the article, that she had a passionate nature. I'd have thought it would be the other way around, and my observation puzzled me. I wondered about myself. I'd just gotten a Little Lady lip gloss from Engelman's children's department, so the jury was still out on what shape it would take on as I used it.

Grandma came downstairs to babysit, and we stood at the front door, waving as my parents walked down the street to the party. Mom and Dad looked swell all dressed up. I wondered if they would come home determined to be more like Rhoda's parents. I wondered if I would like it if they did.

We sat on the porch for a bit, watching the cars whiz by. Motion was the order of the day. Even Father Ryan had noticed it. He'd given a sermon at Sunday Mass about how we all were going places, drawing a travel analogy to explain how it was better for Catholics because we were blessed with the one true faith. As he saw it, we were all traveling through life, hopefully with heaven as our final destination, but Catholics were riding on the *Queen Mary* while Protestants were traveling in a rowboat. He hadn't thought to include cars and foot traffic, but I added them on my own. I drew my own conclusion that it was better to ride than to walk and worried that my parents were lagging behind.

Grandma and I tucked Molly into bed. I got comfortable in mine, intending to read, but I guess I dozed off, because when I woke, our house was dark except for the kitchen. The radio was playing, turned down low. My parents were talking, and the clanking of their spoons told me they were having their evening cup of tea.

Bits of conversation drifted my way.

"That was a terrific mural you painted," said Mom. And then, "Rhoda McMahon is 'the hostess with the mostest,'" a statement I knew from my magazine reading referred to Pearl Mesta, a lady famous for throwing splashy parties.

Dad murmured something about stuffed shirts. And Mom named some people who she said were three sheets to the wind. Then they laughed. They sounded glad to be back home from the McMahons, and not a bit different from when they'd left for their night of glamour.

The radio began to play a song with French words, sung by a man with a voice like warm caramel sauce on an ice cream sundae.

Dad's parents spoke French all the time when they didn't want me to know what they were saying, but Grandma had explained to me that "Je vous aime beaucoup" means "I love you very much," so I understood what Nat King Cole, the man on the radio, was singing. When I got up from my bed and peeked into the kitchen, I saw that my parents were dancing.

My Name Is Ted

Breathing out and in is what sustains the body, but it is focusing on details that supports the sinking mind. A brilliant shaft of sun in the noon hour, the pinkness of 5:00 am that accompanies the Worden's dairyman on his springtime route up Walnut Street, the white candles that see themselves reflected in Mother's copper bowl on our dining room table all please me in the way that others feel toward a lover's kiss or a baby's mewling cry.

I am not an artist, though I might have become one if I'd tried. I have viewed my surroundings with a chiaroscurist's eye for light and dark since I was old enough to take my first short steps and to call the things I saw by their proper names.

In his last year of life, my father sat each day with his slippered feet propped on the fender of our parlor stove. The brown metal kerosene heater had an oily smell, and the linoleum rug beneath it remained cold, its pale cabbage roses filmed with soot. Our fox terrier, Lady, sat beside Dad, her muzzle tucked beneath his liver-spotted hand. Knowing Lady as I did, I suspected this was as much for warmth as for affection. Even in June, the room felt chill.

In our kitchen pantry on the bottom shelf, a bottle of Four Roses sat flanked by two shot glasses. It lay in easy reach yet out of sight if someone should drop by without warning. The brown bottle glowed like Lady's eyes when she was glad, discernable to me even in the dim light that crept in to it through the pantry's white-paneled door.

Dad took precisely one drink every evening at exactly five. I'd pour the shot and bring it to him on our blue tin tray. Niagara Falls, the rushing view of it from the Canadian side, was lithographed on it in bright primary colors. The tray was a souvenir, Dad said, chosen by my mother on their honeymoon.

"May you be in heaven half an hour before the devil knows you're dead," Dad toasted me every night, tossing back the whiskey with a single gulp. A Kerryman from the south of Ireland, Dad pronounced *devil* as a three-syllable word, his rolling brogue echoing the cadence of Niagara's roiling falls.

At Easter and on Christmas Eve, Dad would invite me to join him, our glasses trayed companions poised above Niagara's blue water. At times like that, Dad turned from mellow to melancholy with prestissimo speed. To avoid his lamentations, I'd learned to be even quicker. On my feet, tray grasped firmly in both hands, I'd call over my shoulder, "I'll just be washing up now."

After I'd rinsed his glass and mine, I'd perform my own ritual. It was one that I practiced every night, filling a juice tumbler with vodka neat from my own supply stored under the kitchen sink. I thought of it as medicine, taken to calm my nerves. After the second glass went down, thoughts that overwhelmed me in the daylight hours began to seem more possible. Perhaps I'd return to teacher's college to finish my diploma. Or I might complete the nurse's training I'd quit after the first six months. I might even marry and keep a house of my own.

Once I'd started on it, nothing ever proved to be what I'd expected. It worried me that I was twenty-nine, but surely there was still time. In a way, keeping house for Dad had proved a blessing, a reason for postponing my life. In school, the nuns had told us that virtue is its own reward. And truly, doing for Dad took up so much time that it left me only a little room for fear.

I couldn't put a name on what it was that haunted me. It wasn't like dreading thunderstorms or worrying about black cats, something the person you'd confide in would understand and perhaps even reward with a nod of "me too." What I felt was more a premonition that before I'd figured out what it was I was supposed to be doing here I'd have come to the end of my time.

Lady clicked to the back door with the too long nails of a dog that gets little exercise and whined to be let out.

"Mud in your eye," I toasted her, draining my glass. As an educated woman, I shudder when I hear a cliché. Yet for something ceremonial as a toast, the old words worn smooth as worry stones by generations past provide a continuity that soothes me like a lullaby.

To the left of our kitchen's back door, the Fulton Market's annual gift calendar read June. Beneath the brightly printed picture of a golden-haired boy pulling a red wagon, the year was blazoned in inch-high numbers: 1947. In the wagon crouched a big gray cat, ears back and bow askew, biding its time for escape. I tore the page off and turned a new leaf to July.

I'd been keeping company with Tim since 1945. We'd met on VJ Day. Tim had been home on leave. His army uniform and the chevron on his sleeve that meant sergeant had caught my eye as we stood side by side that day on the Waterbury Green. We were lost together in the large crowd, watching a sailor in his uniform of blue middy blouse and bell bottoms climb up onto the brass horse at the south end of the Green above the Carrie Welton Fountain.

People were wild that day, crying, laughing, shouting. They were kissing people they didn't even know, celebrating victory over Japan. Theirs was an excess of emotion I eschewed yet at the same time admired. Over by the granite clock with four faces, two Gold Star mothers whom I recognized from my neighborhood stood apart and silent.

I later learned that Tim himself had been in combat. When he told me he had a Purple Heart at home in his bureau drawer, it struck me as such a funny thing to say that I'd laughed. With a disapproving look, he'd set me straight. And when I'd wheedled and coaxed enough, Tim took me home with him to see it, nearly two years to the day from the time we'd met.

I'd worn my new white hat. It gave me confidence as I sat in Mrs. Malloy's painfully clean parlor, making small talk. A tiny, wiry woman from the West of Ireland, she'd eyed me critically as a match for her only child. When I opened the velvet box Tim brought out to me, I expected to see something bright, like a jeweled brooch, not at all the somber article on a violet ribbon that lay inside. It was just one more disappointment.

"The days of man are but as grass," sighed Mrs. Malloy, standing to dust the top of the picture of Jesus with a crown of thorns around his heart. It hung above the couch, and I ducked as she reached above me to swipe at it with the corner of her apron.

"We'll be off now, Mother," Tim told her. And to me he whispered, "Let's go for a drink."

In Waterbury in 1947, most folks didn't use cars to get around town. We caught the bus downtown, linking hands as we made a run for it. My hat slipped down over my eyes. Tim kissed me as he bent to straighten it, his fingers catching in its veil.

"You may kiss the bride," he joked. "Shall we, Ted? I'd say that it's about time."

It was Sister Maurita at Saint Mary's School who'd told us that the light of the body is in the eyes. And although it was something she'd read out of the New Testament to our confirmation class, it had the ring of truth. I'd seen for myself the bright look of anticipation, the heated glow of rage, the melting light of love. And every one of them supported Matthew the Evangelist's observation.

Kindling in Tim's gaze, I answered yes.

"I'll be your bride next June," I said. I liked the over-the-top drama of the phrase. It was something I'd heard once in a movie and longed ever since to say myself. Waiting for happiness was in my blood. I savored promised treats. Fourth of July sparklers, a heart-shaped box of chocolates on Valentine's Day, the crisp five-dollar bill tucked into my birthday card by Great Uncle Pat all gained in my eyes from anticipation.

Our bus left us downtown at Exchange Place by the Green. The gray stone clock was striking six. It was Thursday night in Brass City, pay day for the factories, and the streets had a party air. We strolled along Bank Street, window shopping. A red dress in the window of Howland-Hughes caught my eye.

"I'd like that," I told Tim.

"I'd rather you in the pink, Teddie. My mother says that only fast girls wear red."

I reached into my purse for a cigarette, struck the match against the brick-front wall of the store. Smoking was a habit of mine that Tim found annoying. I exhaled at him, breathing fire.

"I'll be the judge of what looks right on me."

As I crushed the match under my heel, I pictured Mrs. Malloy's smug face. It was the flash of the color red that enchanted me, its "look at me" lure that emphasized to the world that I could do as I chose.

When we reached Drescher's Restaurant I ordered a whiskey neat, and when I'd downed it, another. When the bartender called "Time, gentlemen," it was midnight, with no chance of getting dinner now. It was too late even to catch the last bus home.

We swayed down Harrison Alley. When I glanced up into the narrow strip of sky over our heads, I felt unbalanced as the moon above us seemed to grow a twin. My spectator pumps and Tim's wing tips moved not quite in unison, as we wrapped our arms around each other's waists. I seemed to walk straighter when I focused on our feet. Tim laughed, saying that since we were on a forced march, I might as well count cadence. I began:

He had done with roofs and men.
Open, time, and let him pass.

That was part of a poem I'd learned in high school, in senior English at Crosby. I couldn't say why it had come to mind. It had nothing to do with us at all. But it got us as far as the Green.

"Walking home will blow the cobwebs away, Teddie." Tim paused by the water trough at the east end of the Green to splash water on his face and hair.

"A grand horse he was," Tim continued, looking up at the statue of Knight. The horse's raised right hoof was a malevolent reminder that he'd kicked a man to death. But his owner, Carrie Welton, had erected the monument anyway as a tribute to her favorite mount, even though the horse's victim had been her father. Perched on the fountain's lip, I trailed my hand through the silky water. My white glove cut through the blackness like a pale fin.

"I may be going blind, Theodora, but I'm no man's fool." Dad was standing at the kitchen door, pointing to my glass. I'd taken one of the little ones from Mother's breakfast set with the matching pitcher. Oranges with bright green leaves danced in and out of checkered orange squares around its rim. My juice, though, was laced with vodka to pick me up after the night before.

Tim had come close to falling over the railing as he'd walked me up the back porch stairs. I'd caught him by his shirt front, and we'd laughed it off.

"Whoa," he'd whispered, squinting against the porch light. Later, in the bathroom mirror, I'd talked the evening over with myself, eyes glittering and lipstick askew. Father and Lady were snoring counterpoint in the next room as I'd blown my reflection a kiss and felt my way down the hall to bed.

"Crashing around at all hours! You were loud enough to wake the dead," Dad had shouted next morning through my closed bedroom door. The brightness in my room was harsh as an Edward Hopper painting. The sharpness of the detail hurt my eyes as I hastened to draw the shade.

"You've no discipline, Theodora. And neither does the lad," Dad continued.

"Ted, Dad. My name is Ted," I answered. I'd changed it as soon as Mother died, at the same time that I'd cut off my long braids.

When her cancer had advanced so far that she could no longer work in the better dresses department of Jones-Morgan, my mother had taken to her bed. In the long mirror of her vanity, I'd braid my hair each morning under her watchful eyes. I disliked my reflection, the brown mole on my left cheek like a hex. Our landlady had told me it was there because my mother had been frightened by a mouse while expecting me. Yet even though Dad had dismissed it as pure nonsense, the mark, contrasted with my mother's own perfection, burned in me like my own fatal disease.

"Come now, Theodora. Let me tie your bows." Mother was proud of her small hands. Her diamond flashed as she fastened the ribbons to bind the ends of my braids. The blue box my mother's ring had come in was lined in white satin like a little nest, with a slit where you'd rest your ring if you could ever bear to take it off. "Kay," read the jeweler's name in swirly golden script. And the store's jingle on WATR radio reminded customers that "It's okay to owe Kay."

Each afternoon on the way home from school, I practiced my jump rope team's favorite chant:

Step on a crack.
Break your mother's back.

And so I'd imagined with satisfaction when Mother first fell ill that I'd been successful, putting an end to her daily orders and relentlessly critical gaze. On the morning Dad came to tell me tearfully that she'd passed, I took her shears and cut away my braids. The little motes of dust that danced in the sun beams that hit them as they lay coiled on the bathroom floor mirrored the lightness I'd felt at their slow fall.

Free of her control, I lived much in my mind, dreamy with the knowledge that I could now do as I pleased. The possible piggybacked on the probable, overriding the prosaic reality of each new day until both sank, too entangled to go on.

When Dad thought me old enough to take my first taste of spirits at Christmas, I'd been delighted to discover that it made even dull people more interesting, enhancing them with an animation that sprang from my own fertile mind.

How welcome Tim's proposal had been to me. I was ready for a change. On our honeymoon, we'd go to Atlantic City. We'd stroll the Boardwalk, toss a bottle with a message in it into the Atlantic Ocean. Back home, we'd set up housekeeping, our mingled laundry hung out to dry in our own backyard. The rest of it was hazy, but I figured to work out the details as I went along.

I was relieved not to have to fret anymore about my future. Clearly marriage was a career of its own, a solid destination.

"My husband fancies a nice lean cut of lamb," I'd tell the butcher, my own ring gleaming as I pointed to the meat case lit by the ceiling light with its wooden paddle fan.

I held Tim's kiss too long.

"Easy, Teddie. Nice girls wait for their wedding night," he reproached me. The appeal of the physical side of love had taken me by surprise, given Mother's cryptic warnings, Dad's grim asides. Tim's mouth on mine, the feeling of his hands moving on my back, brought my longing for the intangible into sharp focus. It was the last move in the waiting game I liked to play, the best prize yet, far above and beyond party favors or candy hearts.

We'd drunk a toast with Dad to our future and continued the party alone in the kitchen after he'd gone to bed. I let Lady out. Moths fluttered around the back door light, their furry bodies pressed against its heat.

"They're drawn to it," Tim slurred, belaboring the obvious in a way I found annoying. I stood inside the screen door and watched him take his leave. At the top of the stairs, he turned to wave good-bye.

Everything we do is a memory in the making, even though it's not always the one you'd like it to be that stays with you till you'd sometimes like to scream. Even now, the smell of geraniums or a man with a particular shade of sandy, curling hair can bring that night right back, if I let it in.

A scrabble of paws on the landing, and Lady's face appeared behind him, a pale moon in the dark well of the staircase. Tim's backward sway took both of them by surprise. The arc of his body as he struggled to keep his balance is what I remember most, and the absence of his cry.

I knelt beside him at the bottom of the stairs, my red dress dragging in the landlady's flower bed, her flowers crushed in disarray. From inside the house, muffled voices rose, and neighbors hurried to turn on their back porch lights. I put my hands over my eyes to shield them from the light's harsh glare, from the brightness that illuminated what I feared to know.

The End Of The Line

"That's it," says the man unloading his pickup truck. "That's all of it. The end of the line."

Betty does not know the name of the man, only that he's come to deliver the personal effects of her childhood friend and mentor. After years of a steady decline at the hands of alcohol, Ted is to be committed to an asylum. The delivery man is not looking so steady himself. She can smell the whiskey on him as she directs him to carry Ted's cedar chest down the hatchway stairs into her cellar.

It's a piece of furniture she remembers well from the old days. Made of walnut, it is dark brown with inlays of birch in a chevron pattern. On its top, dead center, is a pale rose, worked in cutout bits of wood veneer.

Women call this type of furniture a hope chest. High school girls buy them downtown in Hadley's to save up sheets and table linens and such for their own first homes as brides. Betty herself has one in her bedroom, a maple one with a carving of a spinning wheel on its front. As Ted's chest leaves the sunny backyard for the basement, Betty can see that its top is ringed with circles from wet glasses set down on it. In the rose's center is a long dark burn from a cigarette.

Betty is home alone today, her daughters Betts and Molly are in school. It's just as well, she thinks. She is not prepared to answer any questions. When the delivery man has gone on his way with the cellar hatch firmly closed behind him, she approaches the chest. It's unlocked, its key lost or misplaced long ago. She presses the metal button that pops the lid and looks inside.

Standing in the cool, shadowy cellar, she is reminded of the Greek myth of Pandora's box. When Pandora lifted the lid of the forbidden box, all the troubles in the world flew out. At its bottom, though, tucked into a back corner, was hope.

"Not in this case," Betty tells herself, surveying the items on the shelf attached to the trunk lid with fold-out hinges. There's a bulging envelope of black-and-white photographs turned sepia with age, a worn blue velvet jewelry store box with an empty slit where a ring once sat, a Red Cross badge, and what looks like a diploma rolled up into a scroll. A lidless Whitman Sampler box holds a pair of brown braids bound at their ends with twine.

"I'll finish this another day," Betty says out loud. She finds she is suddenly robbed of the energy she had only an hour earlier. Upstairs, revived by a fresh cup of coffee, she tries to put the morning aside and continue with her day.

"I saw the delivery man," says Cora, Betty's mother-in-law, coming downstairs from her part of the house.

"He brought Ted's trunk," she replies.

"Where is she now?" Cora asks.

"Saint Mary's Hospital. They're saying that she has a wet brain."

"Will you go to visit her?"

"I'll give it till the end of the week," Betty tells her. "I'll go on Saturday." After a minute, she adds, "Maybe she'll ride out of this. The doctors could be wrong."

Cora knows the back story to Ted and Betty. She's heard it so often that it's become a series of set pieces: "The Christmas Doll," "The Trip to See the Shirley Temple Movie," "The New White Shoes for Betty's First Holy Communion." All these delights came to Betty courtesy of Ted. And so it's no surprise to hear Betty conclude, "She was good to me."

Cora lingers to see if Betty shows signs of heading to the basement. Her curiosity about the contents of the chest is killing her. But she can see that this is not about to happen.

"Call if you need me. I'll be upstairs," she says and is gone as quickly as she first appeared.

Betts and Molly don't discover the chest until Saturday. A rainy afternoon sends them down the narrow basement staircase to the land of discarded chairs and toys, all arranged on a flowered rug that was once in Cora's parlor.

"Mom!" they shriek. "Mom!"

"I know all about it, girls," Betty answers. "Don't touch it. The lid is heavy and dangerous. It could cut your head off if it falls on you."

Danger is a deterrent for the moment, and Betts and Molly dance around the chest, giggling and making throat cutting gestures with their fingers until the game gets old. When they go upstairs for the night, the hope chest is left behind them in the dark.

It's 10:00 pm, and everyone in the house is asleep. Everyone, that is, but Betty. Sitting in the kitchen's platform rocker, she lights a cigarette and thinks of Ted. Betty has seen the movies: *The Snake Pit*, starring Olivia de Havilland, about a woman who finds herself in an asylum with no memory of how she got there, and *I'll Cry Tomorrow*, the tale of Lillian Roth's alcoholic downward spiral.

All the nurses at the convalescent home when Betty worked there went to the movies in a group. They thought of those evenings at the Palace Theater as research, she recalls, though it was more like a girls' night out. Those were Betty's best times, when she was working, and she wishes she could do it again. But Rob wants her home now that there are two children in their family. Being housebound has made her nervous, and smoking is their family doctor's solution to what he calls a common case of housewife jitters.

"I'm a Democrat in a house full of Republicans," she says out loud, as if that explains how she differs from Rob and his family. But she knows it is not that simple. She wonders about Ted, if she'd come to feel uneasy all the time too.

"I hope I don't go crazy," she tells their calico cat, curled up beneath the radiator. Stubbing out her cigarette, she goes to bed.

On Saturday afternoon, Betty catches the downtown bus across the street in front of Delaney's Drugstore. She's wearing heels and her brown tweed coat. Her fall hat is brown felt, with a green feather. It's a short walk up to the hospital. The admissions lady directs her to the third floor, where she finds Ted alone in a four-bed ward.

"Don't excite her," says a nun in the starched white habit of the Holy Ghost Sisters. "We've had to sedate her. She's been very loud."

But Ted is quiet when she sees Betty. Her brown eyes glitter in the overhead light.

"Hello," she says. "Have you come to tea?"

"It's me, Ted. It's Betty. I've come to see you." As she approaches the bed to kiss her cheek, Betty sees the restraints. Ted's arms are hidden beneath a straight jacket. How alert her eyes are as she replies.

"Sure, I know you." The intensity with which she adds "Untie me and we'll have a chat" causes Betty to take a step backward.

"She raved," Betty tells Cora that night. "Nothing she said made any sense. When I said good-bye, she was calling for a drink from the bucket by the door. There wasn't a bucket, though. It was the wastebasket she saw." Betty sighs as Cora pats her shoulder.

That night, sleepless again, Betty opens the chest. She lifts out a smocked christening dress trimmed with lace and a tatty stone marten fur piece with beady glass eyes and dangling feet and tails. There's more in the hope chest, but she can't face it. She leaves the fur piece on a chair where she has laid it aside.

"Can I wear it tonight for Halloween?" asks Betts. Her original plan, to go as Cinderella, is changing. "I could go as a rich old lady instead. You know, like the one you used to work for."

"No. There are probably germs on that thing. Leave it alone."

Molly carries it into the living room. Betty can see her making it walk across the carpet, growling softly as she works its little legs.

"I'll take that," she says, coming up behind dark-haired Molly, whose vivid imagination has been commented on by her kindergarten teacher. She's been costumed since breakfast for trick or treating, dressed as a yellow cat.

Betty and Rob talk as they walk the girls up one side of the street and down the other.

"Ted's doctor didn't want to consult with me, but she has no next of kin. I persuaded him by saying that I'm a nurse. The doctor told me she's become a menace to herself. Her delirium tremens is severe. And her brain isn't coming back."

To Betty, this is a horror story that rivals anything Halloween has to offer. But Rob tells her that Ted brought it on herself. He means, of course, that no one forced Ted to drink.

Neither of them voices the thought that it was Betty's father's episodes of drinking during her childhood that made Ted's kindnesses so important to the little girl she was.

"Betts and Molly are having fun tonight," Betty says, veering away from further discussion. She reaches into Molly's candy bag for something chocolate, pulls out a Hershey's bar, and eats it in a couple of bites.

November passes in a flurry of days, the school pageant where Betts must come up with a Pilgrim hat, the usual Thanksgiving dinner where Betty must employ the wisdom of Solomon, dividing herself between Rob's mother's dinner and her own mother's celebration because Rob likes his mother's cooking best.

Betty knows that Ted has left Saint Mary's and is now at Connecticut Valley Hospital, it's always at the back of her mind. But it's not till Christmas decorations begin to appear downtown that it floods the front of her mind in a wave of nostalgia.

"I'll empty the trunk today," she tells Cora.

"I'll go with you," Cora replies.

In the glare from the dangling overhead light bulb, they take out some unworn slips and nightgowns that seem to have been part of a trousseau, the Purple Heart from Ted's fiancé who passed away before they could marry, a box of unsent Christmas cards, some crocheted doilies, and a scrapbook. Probably the photos in the envelope were intended to be placed in the book, but all its pages are blank.

"Well, that's that," says Cora. "What will you do next?"

"I think I'll go to see her," Betty says. She's just recently gotten her driver's license, and having it has done her a world of good. Even if the car simply sits in the backyard all day, it makes her day seem so much better to have the option of going wherever she'd like without waiting for Rob to drive her.

All the way to Middletown, Betty concentrates on the route, trying not to anticipate what she'll find. The attendant at the asylum guides her through a series of locked metal doors to the day room, where she finds Ted in a gray dress. Ted is bent over a little wooden block with rubber-tipped pegs at equidistant intervals. It's a loom, and Ted is weaving a pot holder with great concentration. She looks up, nods politely, and goes back to her work.

"We tried her on leather first," explains the attendant. "But the loops for belt making were too frustrating to her. And of course, we'd have had to find something other than a buckle to finish it off if she'd completed it. Sharp metal would be out of the question for her."

It's awkward standing there in the day room in her winter coat, waiting for a conversation that she sees will never happen. Betty fidgets with the clasp on her pocketbook, doing her best to avoid eye contact with Ted's fellow patients.

"She doesn't talk much even to us," the attendant says. "Don't feel bad about leaving. We'll take good care of her."

"Good-bye, Ted," Betty says. The attendant has told her it would be better not to make physical contact, so she does not kiss her.

"You can be sure we'll give her your gift," says the attendant, referring to the red cardigan Betty has brought along as a Christmas offering. They walk back through the series of doors. Betty is signed out and knows it is for the first and last time. She won't be coming back to Middletown. The Ted she knew is gone.

On Saturday night, Betty walks up Willow Street to confession. She kneels behind the maroon velvet curtain to tell her woes to Father Ryan on his side of the wooden grate.

"She was good to you, of course, my child," he begins. "But no doubt you helped her as well. We are all occasions of grace for each other. And while it distressed you to see her, keep in mind that your friend was suffering. And now she is not suffering any more."

Betty lights a candle for Ted in front of the Blessed Sacrament and a second one for herself, then walks home. The cold night air seems to promise snow. When she opens her front door, she finds Molly in the living room, dancing to a phonograph record turned up loud. It's her brand-new one of a Christmas song that is allegedly sung by three chipmunks. Their squeaky little voices drive Betty crazy at the best of times. It's the last thing she wants to hear tonight. She'd like to put on her slippers, light a cigarette, and brood over recent events.

She feels like Alice in Wonderland, pulled backward through the knothole. Her past has receded so thoroughly that it seems viewed through the wrong end of a telescope, and it is visible now to her alone. Instead, she is here, surrounded by her own family, who clamor for her attention.

It occurs to Betty that the action in the living room is better for her tonight than silence would be and that, for the most part, her life is what she'd dreamed about back in the days when her favorite thoughts began with "When I grow up."

"Let me get out of my coat," she says, stalling for a bit of time. She has a lot to think about, but it can wait. Betty unzips her fleece lined boots and takes Molly on her lap.

"It feels like snow tonight," she tells the girls. "Let's ask your father if we can get our Christmas tree tomorrow after Mass."

Betts and Molly go to the front window to see if the snow has started yet. Their glee eases something in Betty. She thinks of what the priest said and of his absolution. Her past is a burden that she has carried for a long time. And it will feel good to finally put it down.

TIME GOES BY

Rob has just finished dismantling three beds, the mahogany double bed and the girls' maple twin beds. They are stacked with their mattresses alongside the bedroom walls and covered with their respective flowered quilts. In the center of the living room and both bedrooms, card tables are set up, surrounded by folding chairs borrowed for the day from Murphy's Funeral Home a few blocks below them on Willow Street.

Betty is covering the tables with starched, crisply ironed tablecloths. Betts follows along behind her mother with little bouquets of flowers in assorted vases and cream pitchers. It's a good thing for her purpose that the downstairs rooms open into each other with a nice flow in their part of the house. Betty is throwing a party for her in-laws' fortieth wedding anniversary, and today is the day.

Upstairs in her kitchen, Cora has been grinding coffee beans from the A&P on Cooke Street. She notices that the little vine in its copper pot above the sink has sprouted. It's a surprise to her that it has actually grown from a kernel of popping corn that Betts planted just for fun. Today is Sunday, and soon, she and Mike will be on their way to Mass.

"Did you sleep okay last night?" she asks her husband as he comes up behind her. Cora got up in the night and looked out the bedroom window that faces the backyard. It frames an ancient, gnarled lilac tree, her favorite daytime view. Often, in the wee hours, she can see the stars so clearly in the black sky. Once or twice, a star has seemed to detach from its group and hover above the lilacs. Cora is convinced these lights are really space ships, but when she said as much to her husband, he told her the men with the nets were going to come and take her away if she kept it up.

"I slept fine," Mike replies warily. Cora decides not to report on last night's visit. If it was indeed little green men, they've gone for now.

"Well, it's a big day for us," she continues. "Celebrating forty years."

"Time goes by," Mike tells her. He pours himself a cup of coffee and gives her a kiss.

Cora has a new dress from Musler-Liebeskind for the party. It's lilac satin with a delicately beaded neckline that looks a bit like the blossoms on her favorite tree. She pins on her corsage of pink rosebuds and tucks a matching flower in the lapel of Mike's dark suit. They went downtown last week to have a picture taken in these very clothes, a kind of dress rehearsal for the party as well as to commemorate the occasion. After Mass, Father O'Toole will bless them. Betty has arranged for it at Saint Margaret's Church, just a few blocks up from their house.

"We'd better take the car to church, old lady," Mike tells Cora affectionately. "You look way too fancy for shank's mare."

Cora's thoughts drift off as the priest turns his back to the congregation murmuring in Latin. She remembers herself at ten, the oldest of eight children, half of whom she named herself with the aid of her mother's pantry. There is Morton, for one, courtesy of a blue canister of salt, and Armand, a little misunderstanding on her part of the name on the baking soda box. Next she recalls her young self, a teen age war bride and mother, Mike away in France, being nearly blown to bits at Chateau Thierry. Cora looks at Mike next to her. He seems not to be thinking about anything at all, save the Mass. For sure he is not remembering the Great War or the Purple Heart tucked away in his top drawer among his handkerchiefs. That first baby, Mike Junior, is forty now, fat and bespectacled. There is a daughter too, named Cora for her mother, and Rob, their youngest child, with whom they share the house.

Cora is about to turn fifty-six, though she feels you'd never know it. She has kept her well-corseted figure and smooth complexion. Rob and Betty and their girls watch as Mike and Cora renew their vows after Mass. Molly is excited with the novelty of this Sunday, the house turned upside down and a big white frosted cake with little bride and groom dolls on top in the pantry. Cora has promised her the figurines for her dollhouse when the party ends.

"Hooray," Molly says, waving her black plush cat at Father O'Toole as he blessed the anniversary couple. Betty hushes her with a look and down the hill they go to put the final touches on the sandwiches and coffee.

You can tell Cora's side of the family from Mike's, hers are what her son Rob has labeled "colorful." The men are short and animated, joking and laughing with each other nonstop about their flashy ties. Cora's tiny dark-haired sisters are all dressed to the nines in bright floral prints with matching costume jewelry. These women are workers of exquisitely embroidered baby clothes and table linens, descended from generations of New England thread mill and fabric mill workers who can easily sew up any garment you might wish to wear. Mike's family, on the other hand, is a reserved and undemonstrative lot for whom life is a serious business. They are dressed in their best dark clothes, more appropriate for a funeral, Rob thinks, grinning to see them seated unaware on the funeral home folding chairs with "Murphy" labels glued on to their metal backs.

"Let's drink toast to the bride," calls Cora's brother Milton, as his wife Henrietta tosses a handful of multicolored confetti that she has brought along concealed in her purse. The toast is ginger ale, there is nothing stronger on Betty's party menu, and so she is surprised and horrified by the sudden, madcap action of confetti sprinkled over her living room rug without so much as a "by your leave."

"That man's an e-jit," Zora tells her daughter with a disapproving glance. "If that stuff gets wet, you'll never get the stain out." Zora means *idiot*, of course. It's her brogue that makes the word sound odd. Betty fully agrees. It's the kind of behavior she's come to expect from a member of Cora's family.

Rob decides to change the subject by bringing out the gift he has created for his parents. He has found two pink china shoe ornaments downtown at Strisik's, about the size of the ones Cinderella wore at the ball. They are dainty little high-heeled slippers with china rosebuds on their toes, rosebuds like the ones in Cora's corsage. Inside each one, he has folded crisp new dollar bills into accordion pleats and tied them together separately with a long pink satin ribbon. The bills are equally divided between each shoe to total forty dollars and will come out together from the shoes in an unbroken succession when the ribbon's end is pulled.

Rob's gift is a hit, as much for Rob's thoughtfulness as for the creativity of it. Rob knows his mother has always wished she'd had a proper wedding with a white gown and bouquet, rather than the hasty wartime ceremony at Saint Francis Xavier with Mike let out for an overnight furlough from the army camped in New Haven, poised to take the train to New York City, a doughboy about to board a troop ship to France. And so he has taken great pleasure in planning this party and from anticipating his mother's delighted reaction.

The two families have warmed up to each other a bit by the time the cake is cut, and over coffee, they laugh and exchange stories. Mike's family has no idea that in just a few short months, in August, a flood will come and remove all traces of their massive three-family house on Riverside Street, as well as two of the men seated here this afternoon. And so they regale each other with stories of the winter the Naugatuck River froze hard enough to skate on and of the time their father walked with them to the roundhouse on Railroad Hill Street to watch the trains go in and out, bright sparks flying from the rails against the evening sky.

Cora's brother Kingsley recaps the motor trip he took last summer with his wife Effie and Cora and Mike along the Mohawk Trail in Massachusetts. They'd had coffee at the famous Hairpin Turn, seen the enormous iron stag that guards part of the trail, and climbed up in a rickety wooden tower for a panoramic view of three states.

"We slept in little cabins like pioneers," Kingsley laughs, although the wooden tourist cabins were more like tiny white dollhouses, Cora recalls. Hers had green shutters and red geraniums in its diminutive window boxes.

"Did you see any bears?" someone asks. Kingsley answers with a pun that Zora recognizes as off-color, but she is too much of a lady to remark on it.

What Cora liked best about the trip were the little gift shops with maple sugar candies shaped like tiny leaves and the pine-needle stuffed pillow she bought for the car. It read "I pine and balsam for you" stamped on its white sacking in forest-green ink.

She'd bought a brightly varnished pine box for Betts with its own tiny brass padlock and key. "Souvenir of the Mohawk Trail" was carved into the box's lid along with a stand of pines. Betts has it in her bureau drawer now; it's a good place for special things like the packet of shamrocks she got from Ireland on Saint Patrick's Day and her silver locket with *B* engraved on it in curly script, special things that you'd want to keep safe as remembrances.

"Another toast," calls Kingsley as he finishes his story:

Make new friends.
But keep the old.

One is silver.
But the other's gold.

Everyone applauds this sentiment, which is old enough to be considered a friend in itself.

"This is a grand party, Cora. It's a regular jubilee," Zora tells her. Zora has not had a proper wedding either, and she is enjoying this party and its fabulous wedding cake with a particular and private zest, although she would never say so out loud.

Betty is more than ready for them all to go home. She has been keeping an eye on the confetti on her rug, and is itching to vacuum it up and put her house back to rights. She's glad she gave the party, but it's nearly five o'clock now, and as she sees it, enough is enough.

"Say, you two never had a real wedding either, come to think of it," Kingsley says.

Betty and Rob were married by a justice of the peace when he enlisted in the navy right after Pearl Harbor. Betty has never examined this chain of hasty weddings before today. She hopes it is not something that is inherited. She'd like Betts and Molly to walk down a church aisle someday wearing long white dresses and veils. She thinks about the three couples and how their marriages have been the product of snap decisions. In her case and Cora's, it was a war that prompted it, and in Zora's, it was the need for a hasty emigration from Ireland, the place her father fondly calls the auld sod. Betty's wedding is the only case where a baby on the way was not thrown into the mix, a point she prides herself on but realizes is better left unvoiced.

If Betty was a student of psychology, she'd know that the idea she is playing with has already been pondered by Carl Jung, whose studies suggested that the unlived lives of the parents shape the lives of their children in mysterious ways. Sometimes, hanging out the wash or lying in bed at night, she plays with the what-ifs in her mind. The various conclusions she reaches depend on her state of mind at that time.

When the last of the family has left, Mike helps Rob set the beds back up, then calls good night as he goes upstairs to his part of the house. Cora has taken off her satin dress and put it on a padded hanger. It will disappear along with Mike's dark suit into the deep front room closet to hang in the cool darkness until its next performance.

The pink china slippers are on the coffee table in the living room. They sparkle in the light from Mike's reading lamp as the anniversary couple think over their day. Cora is remembering her dilemma forty years ago, Mike Junior on the way and his father heading off to war. How frightened she had been to tell her parents.

"Mon Dieu," her tiny French mother had exclaimed, twisting her apron. But her grim Methodist father had dismissed her with the words "Well, my little girl, you have burned yourself and now you must sit on your blister."

She looks around the parlor at her flowered Castro convertible couch and the heavy-gilded mirror above it, thinks of her mahogany twin beds with their carved pineapple finials in the bedroom, and of the roast she will make for next Sunday's dinner. She and Mike did marry, and it has all worked out. They have even moved away from Mike's family in the Brooklyn part of the city, and her grandchildren are asleep below them in the little house.

"Well, I'd say it is time for bed," Mike tells her, turning out the light.

When Cora wakes in the night as she usually does, sure enough one of the stars seems to have drawn awfully close to the lilac tree. She thinks about a postcard her brother Kingsley sent last winter, back when he took a trip to Florida. Cora calls it "up in Florida" despite Rob's repeated explanations that Florida is actually "down" from Connecticut.

The postcard had a sandy beach and a sky as blue as the ocean beneath it. There was a border of oranges on it and a smiling alligator in one corner. Across the bottom of the card, in orange script, it read, "Come on down! The weather is fine!"

Cora tells herself that if the star she is watching should prove to be a space ship looking for a place to land, she knows exactly what she would say to the little green men.

She'd tell them, "Come on down. The world is fine."

WHAT I LEARNED FROM READING FANNIE HURST

The summer that I was twelve, I discovered a book hidden on the closet shelf of my grandmother's spare bedroom. A soiled paperback, it looked as if it had been chewed rather than read. The book had been wedged behind some yellow organdy tieback curtains and a bag of wooden clothespins. Grandma's winter hat crowned the arrangement, its black feather curled like a beckoning finger.

It was an amazing, out-of-place discovery, like finding a Cracker Jack toy in a can of peaches. My grandparents did not read books. What they read was the morning *Republican* and the evening *American* newspapers or back issues of the *Kerryman,* mailed to America in a cardboard tube by Grandma's sister Una in Killarney. I suspected that this book had been left behind by my cousin Jimmy.

He'd spent all spring and part of the summer at my grandparents' house, sleeping in their spare room's single Hollywood bed with its heart-shaped gray vinyl headboard. He'd kept his underwear in the rose-printed cardboard chest of drawers with the white wooden pulls that I'd always considered my own property, hung his pants and shirts behind the flowered cretonne curtain that served as a closet door in the tiny room that I thought of as mine.

As I saw it, weekends at my grandparents' house were all mine. And I resented my cousin's intrusion into territory I'd claimed as my own.

The fact that Jimmy had left his home was puzzling to me because I'd overheard that it was due to a tramp. In the adventures of *Nancy Drew: Girl Detective,* tramps were usually down on their luck men, hoboes, and vagrants. In Nancy's adventures, they proved, more often than not, to be heirs to great fortunes who'd gotten themselves misplaced due either to amnesia or a villain's evil plan. A tramp's connection to my cousin Jimmy was inexplicable.

The first clue to the situation had come by phone. On that afternoon in April, my mother lifted the receiver and sank into our kitchen's platform rocker, signaling me with hands and pointed foot to bring her cigarettes and the beanbag ashtray. The ashtray meant a lengthy conversation was expected. I lingered just out of sight in the next room, but my mother's side of the conversation proved disappointingly brief.

"No," she said, drawing out the vowel in an amused way. Then more firmly, "No! I never . . ." When she said the name of the person at the other end of the line, I knew it was Jimmy's wife.

My mother had always been generous with what she referred to as "a piece of her mind." But now, perhaps for the first time ever, I saw her at a loss for words. When she hung up the phone, she smoked three cigarettes in a row, rocking the chair occasionally with one foot.

That night, when my father came home from work, my mother beckoned him to the bedroom and closed the door.

"My cousin Jimmy is at Mom's," I heard. "Left her for a tramp." My mother continued with a sob, "Blames me . . . says I never liked her!" Dad laughed.

"What do you mean, she's right!" My mother's voice grew loud with indignation.

Next day, my mother explained that Jimmy had moved into Grandma's spare room and that my weekly sleepovers were on hold indefinitely. I counted on those weekends away. My mother's mother was the queen of laissez-faire. She let me read as much as I liked and never reprimanded for twisting my hair as I read. Best of all, she never suggested that fresh air would do me good.

"When will he go home?" I asked.

"I'll let you know when it happens," Mom replied.

"But why is he there in the first place?"

"Someday you'll be grown up, and then you'll understand."

My mother had a look, when she told me this, which I thought of as "the look." It meant that it was time for me to change the subject.

I'd intended to read Nancy Drew's *The Secret in the Old Attic* that afternoon. But having found myself in the middle of a real live mystery had given me something to think about. I retreated to my room. I wasn't allowed to sit on my bedspread, so I occupied myself by rearranging my bookcase. On the bottom shelf, still in the plain brown wrapper it had worn when it appeared in our mailbox one morning, sat a little booklet my mother had sent away for. *Growing Up and Liking It* was its title. It had come free, courtesy of the Modess Company, makers of sanitary napkins. I wasn't using their product yet myself, but my mother believed in being prepared.

"This is for you. Read it," Mom had said, handing it to me. Maybe it was the plain brown wrapper, but that book had the feel of something clandestine. I'd hidden it on my shelf behind *Lives of the Saints* for another time. But suddenly, now seemed the right time to scout out some information on the matter of what Modess termed growing up.

I made myself comfortable on the rug and leaned against the wall. I slit open the wrapper and began with the diagrams. Inside me, I discovered, was a maze of organs as complicated as the "Can You Find Your Way Out?" puzzle in the cartoon section of the Sunday comics. Those usually featured a fuzzy animal, maybe a rabbit, at one end and a carrot at the other, or variations on a pirate and his treasure chest. In this instance, though, it was an egg-filled ovary sending one of its members down a fallopian tube to the uterus.

Modess explained that when the egg reached its goal, it waited to be fertilized. If the egg was out of luck that month, you'd need the Modess Company's product. I examined the diagram of the harness that came along with the pad. It cinched on the way Grandma's garters fastened to her stockings. It seemed like a practical joke that I'd have to walk around for a week out of each month with this contraption concealed between my legs. I wondered if Nancy Drew knew about it.

A bigger mystery was exactly how the baby process happened in the first place. I flipped through the manual all the way to the end, but that information was not included. In the "Questions and Answers" section, I read about issues that had never occurred to me.

"Can I go horseback riding with my period?"

"Certainly," said the book. "Exercise is beneficial." There was a grainy photo of a girl in a black velvet hat and jodhpurs jumping a white fence on an enormous horse with a braided mane and tail. The only horse I'd ever been on had been firmly anchored to the carousel at Lake Quassapaug Amusement Park. The idea that this confident rider could be me seemed as implausible as the whole egg process itself.

Further information included the notice that hair washing during this time was still okay. The book made a plea for maintaining good hygiene, euphemistically referred to as personal daintiness. There was even a warning about avoiding inquisitive dogs. The book concluded with a coupon to return by mail for my very own complimentary napkin belt and hearty congratulations from the Modess Company on becoming a young lady. I put the book back in the bookcase and went upstairs. Privacy was nonexistent at our house, and the only room with a lock on it was Grandma's bathroom. I shot the barrel bolt on the door and opened the linen closet. Probably this room had been a sewing room when the house was built back in the Civil War era, because its deep closet had a long mirror set into its door. The floor-length window on the north side looked out into the side yard of the three-family house next door.

One of our neighbors was a handsome, dark-haired teenaged boy. I'd seen him kissing his girlfriend once, from this very window. He'd leaned her against the stone wall in front of his house. She'd bent one leg at the knee, her ballet-slippered foot balancing on thin air. When she ran her hands along his back, her red-painted fingernails were bright against his white shirt. Just as he'd moved his mouth from her lips to her throat, my mother had appeared behind me and yanked down the shade.

"That tramp," she'd said. "She'll come to no good."

While I was thinking things over, I rummaged in the closet's shelves and removed four washcloths. I bunched them together, two for each side, and arranged them under my white sweater to see how I'd look if I ever grew breasts. Both grandmothers and my mother as well had enormous ones, but so far, my only curve was my stomach.

"It's just puppy fat," I'd been told. "You'll grow out of it." I hoped that they were right. I added a dash of red lipstick for effect and turned in the mirror from front to side. The washcloths were clearly square and at odds with my white bucks and plaid pedal pushers, so I refolded them and returned them to their shelf. It would not do to spend too much time behind closed doors at my house.

"What are you doing?" would be the first question, but I preferred it to its companion question, "What are you thinking?" I longed for my room at Grandma's house where I could lie on the rumpled chenille bedspread and dream.

In late July, Jimmy returned to his own home. My parents drove me to my grandparents' that Friday night to spend the weekend.

"Boy, tonight's a scorcher," Dad said. The windows on his Ford were rolled all the way down as we passed the Scovill factory on East Main. The heat made the asphalt road look baked and gave the brick building a shimmery halo against the setting sun. Men on break from the machines hung halfway out the open windows, straining to catch a breeze. Their cigarette tips hung from their lips, glowing red against the dark interior. Every time that we passed that place, I prayed that I would never have to work there behind those elaborate iron gates.

"You'd better marry someone rich then" was my mother's advice. "A man trap can write her own ticket." I didn't know what a man trap was, exactly, but surmised that it was something like the woman who had ensnared my cousin Jimmy. If so, it seemed to me to be the opposite of Jimmy's wife, to whom the family always referred, in the same breath as her name, as a "good girl."

When we reached my grandparents' house, I went straight to my room, leaving the grown-ups in the kitchen to talk over tea and cake. I could hear them clinking their teaspoons against their cups, no doubt adding cream and sugar to a beverage that only the Irish would not consider too hot a drink for a July night.

"Met her in a bar," I heard my mother say. "She thought she'd latch on . . ."

"A crafty thing she was," Grandma said softly.

"Well, she got hers," added Dad. A soft murmur of assent followed then silence.

Meanwhile, I was hunting through the closet for the tiebacks to Grandma's organdy summer curtains. It had occurred to me that they would make better padding for my imaginary breasts than my other grandmother's washcloths. And I would have all the time in the world this weekend to study their effect in the wavy old mirror that hung above the cardboard chest of drawers.

When I pulled them down from the shelf, the paperback book came with them. It was called *Back Street*, and its author was Fannie Hurst. The cover had a scarlet background and showed a dark-haired woman in a dingy white slip standing alone in a shabby bedroom. She stood at its single window, parting the curtain with her hand. Her nails were painted red, and she was wearing matching lipstick.

Behind the woman was a rumpled, unmade bed, something you would never find at my house. Down the street outside the window, a man in a dark suit and a hat like the one my father wore to Mass on Sunday was slinking along beneath the street light. It was obvious that he was heading for the woman in the slip. I knew when I saw it that this was the kind of book my mother would confiscate in a heartbeat. I drew the closet's curtain around me and began to read.

Back Street told the story of a woman who spooned with men and acted fly. I had never heard those terms before, but I found them self-explanatory. When I reached the part where the woman kissed the traveling man, I felt a twinge of excitement. I'd practiced kissing lately myself. My partner had been a large brown teddy bear I'd won at school for selling the most chocolate bars. Teddy's fuzz had come off on my blue jersey, and the question of whether to close my eyes or gaze into his black button ones was as problematic as the arrangement of my tongue in his flapping red corduroy mouth.

By page four, the woman in the story was feeling the sap running in her body and admiring the contours of her own breasts. I felt a kinship with her and believed that this book I'd found would finally clue me in to what I wanted to know.

"We're leaving now, come and say good night," my father called from the bottom of the stairs. I pushed the book under my mattress and went down.

"You look flushed," my mother said. "I hope you're not coming down with something."

"I'll go right to bed," I countered, afraid she'd take me home with her, away from the book. I stayed awake that night, reading. My grandparents were the kind of folks who snored their way to dawn. They did not see the lamp behind my door making a pale streak of light across the striped hall runner. And every hour on the hour, the Forestville clock struck a throaty series of bongs to let me know the time.

Time was passing on *Back Street* as well. At first, the woman and the man experienced tides of ecstasy that made them feel great. But it wasn't long before the man began to change. Adultery was defined, and sure enough, it was the sixth commandment that the man and woman were breaking. Things stopped being romantic.

"I know I walk the back streets of your life," the woman whimpered to the man who had grown cold. I knew that if it had been my mother, she would have slapped him. More to the point, my mother would never have been there in the first place. One of her favorite adages was about how a man would never buy a cow if milk was cheap. She'd said it while discussing the arrangement of a divorced woman who lived on the next street with her boyfriend, and I'd heard it enough to figure it out for myself.

By 6:00 am, I was bleary-eyed from lack of sleep, and the *Back Street* woman, whose name was Ray, was dead. Her death made feel like crying. I wished I could talk about the story and why this had happened. But I was out of luck because the story was something I had not been supposed to read in the first place. I wondered if the same thing had happened to my cousin Jimmy's lady friend.

"Tramp" had the ring of sin. It was a word that Father O'Dea might thunder from his pulpit at Sunday Mass. But when I thought about Jimmy's mystery girlfriend, I saw that it could apply to any woman who loved a man as Ray did. It was a frightening thought that it could even be me when I grew up and that lipstick and kissing could be the beginning of a woman's downward spiral. I put the book back where I'd found it, buried on the closet shelf along with the carefully folded curtain tiebacks.

On Sunday afternoon, Jimmy and his wife came to visit. Grandma asked me to pour the ginger ale into her red-checkered glasses with the Scottie dogs on them, and I fanned out the Oreo cookies across the milk glass plate with a picture of a jaunting car in its center. Grandpa went into the living room and came back with his can of tobacco that he kept behind the couch. He and Jimmy rolled smokes for themselves. Jimmy's fingers shook as he tamped the paper closed and stuck out his tongue to seal his cigarette closed.

Grandma fussed over the gas stove even though my grandfather made his usual comment about watched kettles never boiling. If she was in a playful mood, Grandma would usually smack him with the flyswatter that hung on the wall by the window. But today's mood was oddly formal. Jimmy paced in the narrow hallway, peering out through the screen door. Only Jimmy's wife was serene. She sat at Grandma's kitchen table like one of Grandpa's plaster statues upstairs on his bureau, with a smile that was hard to figure out. Despite the heat, her white blouse was buttoned all the way to her neck. Her gold wedding band glinted in the afternoon sun, throwing little squares of light on the kitchen's walls.

"Let's get out of here and cool down," Jimmy said to her abruptly. "We'll take the kid to the park."

I started to get into the car's backseat, but Jimmy stopped me.

"Sit up front with us," he said. As we stood face to face I saw that his blue eyes were exactly the color of mine. The freckles on the bridge of his nose were patterned like mine too, on a light skin that would never turn to tan.

"She's riding shotgun," Jimmy told his wife. She hesitated for a moment, then held the passenger side front door open for me. I slid in quickly, rucking up the skirt of my dress. The Buick's front seat was red hot from being in the sun. When Jimmy shifted the car into drive, his muscles flexed beneath the rolled up sleeves of his white shirt.

"Light me a cigarette, will you?" he asked his wife. She reached over, took it from his breast pocket, and put it between her lips. She pushed the cigarette lighter in on the car's dashboard, lit it from the glowing metal tip, and put it in Jimmy's mouth. Jimmy's wife had always made a point of not smoking, so this cigarette-lighting routine was clearly something new for them. We rode in silence to the park. I could smell the Pond's soap my cousin had washed with mingled with his Old Spice aftershave. My dad had the same stuff at home in our medicine chest, reserved for special occasions.

The strangest feeling went right up inside me, like I wanted something but didn't know what it was. I'd eaten lunch, so I knew that I wasn't hungry. It was the same kind of yearning I'd felt reading *Back Street*, the romantic parts of Ray's story before it all went wrong.

I twisted on the front seat, trying to get my skirt tucked back down between me and the hot leather upholstery. Jimmy's wife's arm had remained extended across the back of the seat after she'd lit his cigarette. But suddenly, I felt it swoop down across my shoulders, as she yanked me toward her.

"Sit up straight and don't lean on your cousin," she said. Her sharp voice was far louder than it needed to be in the confines of Jimmy's car. Then in a softer tone, like the one my mother used on me to get me to run to the corner store when I'd rather be reading, she added, "You're the only woman I'll ever let get between me and my husband. Right, honey?"

Jimmy's hands tightened on the Buick's steering wheel, and his face and neck got red. But he kept his eyes on the road and didn't say a word.

I didn't say a word either. I wondered if Jimmy's wife had been able to tell that I'd been stuffing curtain ties under my jersey and reading a book about a woman who did things with a man who wasn't her husband, things that weren't nice. I smoothed my skirt around me as best I could, and tugged it until it covered my knees.

DANCING ON THE MOON

We were playing paper dolls on my friend Betts's shady front porch when her grandmother called down to us that our Saturday morning cartoons were about to start.

"Hop to it, girls. Bugs Bunny is on his way!"

The TV at Betts's house was upstairs in the part where her grandparents lived. At my house, TV was still a dream for the future. We settled in on the flowered couch with juice and cookies, put our feet up on the red leather hassock, and prepared to be entertained.

Bugs and his nemesis, Elmer Fudd, along with Mighty Mouse, caped superhero of the animal kingdom, ruled prime time. But on occasion, the TV station would trot out old cartoons from earlier, silent movie times to fill in blank spots in its programming. Waltzing flowers and twittery little birds were standard fare for these stories. But one memorable Saturday, something different happened. The most amazing cartoon that I had ever seen came on. It was called *Dancing on the Moon*, and it began with the arrival of a wobbly winged twin engine plane that landed in a grassy field.

"Tonight! Dancing on the Moon!" read the sign the airplane pilot planted beside his craft's gangplank. And from all points on the compass, cartoon animals stepped out and up in twos to board it, just like Noah's Ark. The story's plot was simple:

They went.

They danced.

They returned.

All night long, the cartoon animals danced together, two-stepping across craters and refreshing themselves occasionally with genteel sips from the flowing Milky Way. Curious moon men peered out from their own little crater homes to watch the festivities. And in the distance, small as a tiny, streaky marble in the black sky, hung planet Earth.

The animals had dressed formally for their night out, the ladies in ball gowns and stoles, the gentlemen in tuxedos. I knew what tuxedos were from movies on *The Early Show* that we sometimes watched after supper. Fred Astaire had worn one to dance to a song called "Putting on the Ritz." And Jimmy Cagney had worn one in a story where he was a New York City gangster. The versatility of the tuxedo amazed me. I'd never seen a real one, of course. My father delivered bread for Reymond's Sunbeam Bakery, and his daily outfit had his name, Billy, circled on his blue shirt in red. The fact that his work shirt matched his blue pants did give Dad a kind of dash. But his uniform was as different from a tuxedo as the Land O'Lakes cheese we melted on our hamburgers was from the Man in the Moon's green cheese.

I imagined a different sort of life for myself from the one I woke up to each morning. Roused by the sound of Dad's work boots on the porch as he took in the morning newspaper, I'd hug my dreams to myself like a favorite toy. I knew from watching TV at Betts's house that there was a big world out there and that it existed just a TV knob away.

Why did the animals come back from the moon? That was my question. I asked Betts's grandmother when I found her in the kitchen making a cake.

"Maybe they missed their mother's cooking," she guessed. "And besides, where would they go to the bathroom up there?"

It was an answer as practical as my own mother's would have been. At my house, the only book where you could look something up seemed to be a hard covered anatomy text my mother had gotten from an aunt who had taken nurse's training. It had colored pictures of all the organs in the human body and explanations of what to expect if one of them played out of tune.

But I knew that there was actually a second reference book in our house, in my mother's nightgown drawer. It was called the *Zolar Book of Dreams*. I felt sure that my mother consulted it each morning when she put on her lipstick and tied on her apron to begin her day. I'd consulted it myself.

"To dream of cats," *Zolar* advised, "means treachery from one you least expect." I hadn't dreamed of cats myself, but I was glad of the heads up.

Next to our telephone was a pad for messages and a pen. The pen was stuck into a red plastic apple with sharp green leaves on either side of its brown stem. If you pulled the stem straight up, it turned out to be the pen. The trick was to twist the pen while you were pulling it. That was what released a tiny bug-eyed green plastic worm from a little hole in the apple's side.

Our house was on Ridgewood Street, one of a long row of three-family houses stacked on both sides of the narrow street. But I knew that there were real apples to be found on Waterbury trees, if you knew just where to look for them. A few blocks below us on a broad curving avenue stood massive, decaying mansions from our city's heyday as Brass Capital of the World.

My favorite house had a black iron fence with spikes on the tops of its gates. From the top of its winding driveway, there was a bird's-eye view of my hometown, its hills, and its factories' smokestacks. The mansion was made of red stone trimmed in black, with a tower on one side like the one where Rapunzel was kept in my fairy tale book. I'd creep up the driveway as often as I could, scoot under the boxwood hedge as pungent as my cat's litter box, and enjoy the view.

"Tuxedos here," I told myself. I longed to get up close and see more, but like Peter Rabbit in Mr. McGregor's cabbage patch, I was shooed off by the gardener whenever he caught sight of me.

All summer long, I visited "my" house, as I thought of the mansion. And I thought of the old woman who lived in it as the queen. She was not alone. There was a white uniformed nurse in a frilly little cap who walked her to the side lawn on sunny afternoons. That's where the rose beds were, and I often observed the cook adding coffee grounds to the dirt around them.

One day, the queen saw me behind her rhododendron, and we spoke.

"Hello," she said. The banality of her salute took me by surprise.

"Good afternoon," I replied, curtseying. It wasn't as effective in my shorts and sneakers as it had been in my school uniform when our class had curtsied to the Mother Superior on report card day. But I took pride in knowing how, as Mother Saint Rose of Mercy had put it, to act like a lady.

The queen's hair was the color of Grandma's cotton balls. It was wound around her head in a braided coronet. Her scalp beneath it showed as pink as my cat's tongue.

"Where did you come from?" she asked. Beneath her left hand, a grizzled Springer spaniel nuzzled close.

"Give the girl your paw, Nelson," the queen murmured. And so I entered my dream world with my hand extended under the blue afternoon sky.

The queen's name was Lucilla.

"Lucilla Couteaux Grenville," she explained, tracing the monogram on her silver tea tray. The swirls of the *L* and *C* twined around the *G* as gracefully as a dance.

"I'm Mary," I told her. "Mary Blonski."

"Too plain," the queen replied. "I shall call you Minette."

"Call me anything but late for supper," my mother joked when I told her about my new name. Pushing the wicker laundry basket with her foot to position it by the open kitchen window, she picked up a handful of my father's socks and leaned out to the clothesline.

"Hand me the clothespins, will you? Some of us have to work for a living."

Lucilla encouraged my visits.

"Do come for tea, Minette." And so most afternoons found me heading up the winding drive past the curtly nodding gardener to the mansion's side lawn where the table was set for two.

"Cook has brought our tray," Lucilla would say in a voice that whispered collusion. "Shall we see what we have today?"

As I whisked off the linen cloth laid across the sandwiches and cakes, Lucilla would sometimes observe, "'Enough is sufficient to the wise.' Euripides, my dear, was never at a loss for words. You must read the classics when you are older. In Greek, if possible. Come, let us begin."

Tiny rounds of white bread spread with unsalted butter held peppery green-stemmed weeds that the queen called watercress. And the sandwiches filled with fish paste smelled like our cat's dinner. I'd hidden the fish one in my sock after the first bite, as soon as Lucilla looked away. The little cakes, though, were wonderful.

"Petit fours, Minette," Lucilla said as she passed the plate.

They looked to me like presents waiting to be opened. White and pink, yellow and pale green, the cakes had frosting ribbons piped on them, ribbons that tied on top in a frosting bow. Inside the petit fours was hard cake that we washed down with our tea. Lucilla sometimes let me pour it from the silver pot with four fat legs that ended in little paws. A heavy-cut glass bowl in the table's center held roses' heads floating in water.

"Cut flowers go further that way," Lucilla explained. "I learned this from a girlhood friend as a clever thing to do when they begin to lose their bloom. One must always practice thrift, Minette. I myself do so at every turn."

At home that night, I floated some dandelion heads in my mother's blue mixing bowl. I set them on top of my bureau in front of the mirror. I was studying the effect when Dad walked by.

"What's with the weeds?" he called from the doorway.

"It makes them go further," I explained.

"Okay," he replied. "But I think the front lawn already has a bumper crop this summer."

I dreamed that night that I was floating through the sky. Everything beneath me looked so small, like a dollhouse seen through the wrong end of a pair of binoculars. *Zolar*'s explanation was confusing. Floating was not listed. But flying was. On page twenty-eight he wrote, "Dreams of levitation indicate that you will soon be free as a bird."

But on page twenty-nine *Zolar* added, "To see things reduced in size means you may aspire to greater things than you can achieve."

Lucilla and I had discussed aspirations the day she took me into the drawing room of her mansion. In that cool, silent room, the French doors were hung with long blue velvet curtains that puddled on the floor. The chairs had animal faces carved at the ends of their dark wooden arms, and a shadowy gold-framed mirror on one wall was long enough to show me my entire self in it.

Above the marble fireplace hung a painting of a dark-haired woman in a white dress that looked a lot like a sheet. She was posed in profile, head down, her extended arms drooping at the wrists.

"Yes. It is I," Lucilla said, following my gaze. "Draw back the curtains to admit the sun, Minette."

"I was eighteen when that was painted," she continued. "It was in Berlin, where I studied with Isadora Duncan at her Grunewald School for New Dance."

"Were you a ballerina?" I asked.

"Pas de tout," she replied in a stern voice. "Not at all. Our style of dance was spontaneous. Flowing. Free. For that particular dance, I performed to Rachmaninoff's 'Variations on a Theme of Corelli.' I employed the running tanagra, the kneeling tanagra. I used my emotions to tell the story. I found my center and circled out from there in the dance."

I couldn't think of anything to say to that, but it didn't seem to matter to Lucilla, gone back in time to Berlin. In our dusty present day location, my nose began to itch.

"'Wherever the feet go, there goes the future,' was dear Isadora's motto," Lucilla mused. "Have you ever thought, Minette, that you might wish to dance?"

At eleven, I was pudgy and shy. My friend Betts had taken tap dancing at the Waterbury Girls' Club, but I'd pretended not to be interested. I was afraid to look silly in front of strangers. Lucilla was a stranger too, when I thought about it. But she was as far removed from me as if she, like the cartoon characters I admired, was on the moon. Her age, her house, and best of all, her plans for me gave me a glimpse of a future in a place where my drawbacks need no longer apply.

"You will, of course, need a robe de danse, Minette. But for now, we will concern ourselves with your music."

A black gramophone with a brass horn on its top and a little brass crank on its side yielded a stack of waxy grooved records the size of dinner plates. Lucilla's classical music sounded as moody to me as the background scores for *The Early Show* movies. But I recognized the "Triumphal March" from *Aida*. That was the tune the eighth-grade girls at my school lock stepped to on their way into the auditorium to graduate each spring. I played Lucilla's records for her, one at a time, until the sky had turned blue gold.

"I've got to go home to supper," I said, stepping through the open French doors onto the side lawn. A swirl of little bats was weaving through Lucilla's apple trees.

"The bats want their dinner too, Minette. You must remember to say 'dinner,' not 'supper.' Supper is for laborers and dogs."

That night, I dreamed of falling. Dad said it was probably the meatloaf, but *Zolar* suggested that it meant things in my world were looking up. One day, I would be a famous dancer. I would be thin, vivacious, and tall. I probably would even have twenty-twenty sight and could throw away my glasses.

"Breakfast was divine," I told my mother next morning, pushing the last of the Cheerios against the side of the bowl to scoop them up. At our kitchen table, we were light years away from Rockcliffe, the name carved into the stone pillars on the sides of Lucilla's gates.

"That's a bit much, Mary," my mother replied. "After all, it's only Cheerios."

"Coffee, madam?" Dad asked her, pouring it into her cup with a flourish.

"Enjoy it while you can at the old lady's house," he said to me. "Just remember that she's in a different world, and your home is here with us."

"What's it like there, anyway?" Mom asked.

I couldn't think of anything in our neck of the woods to compare it to, to say what it was like. Rockcliffe was simply itself. What I replied was, "I might learn how to dance."

"You mean you'll go to the Girls' Club to take tap dancing this September, Mary?" Mom had been after me for ages to go there after school with Betts.

"Lucilla is going to teach me a different kind of dance," I told her. "She says I have potential. Mom, can I change my name to Minette?"

"Jesus. Where did you get that one?" Dad said. "It sounds like French for Minnie Mouse."

My parents had lost interest in the conversation, so I went out onto the back porch. The sky stayed so light and pretty summer evenings when the sun was going down. All those mingled colors, pink and yellow and blue, made me feel restless. I went back inside for a Three Musketeers bar and though it was billed as big enough to break in three, I ate it all myself.

At Lucilla's, my dance lessons had progressed to the point where she felt ready to set the moves to music.

"Schubert's 'March opus 40, number 4' for you," she decided. "The light trotting. A springing run. Leap. Leap. Run."

Around the lawn I went as Lucilla called out the different steps.

"Now for your costume," she said. "Come with me."

On the upstairs hall landing, the windows were hung with lace.

"Get up on the window seat, Minette, and take one down. We'll spread the others out, and no one will know the difference," she told me. The curtain was as pretty as a bride's veil, despite the dust sifting from it.

"My daughter Monica wore such a veil for the first of her marriages," Lucilla said, as if she'd read my mind. "Dear Monica. So spirited. Although I never could convince her to dance."

Over tea, we discussed how the dance would look when I was in costume. I held my pinkie finger out when I lifted my teacup, just as Lucilla had instructed me. Next afternoon, when I arrived at Rockcliffe, there was a long white car in the driveway in front of the mansion. It was a limousine with little white shades in its windows. The shades had tassels on them to pull them up and down over the tinted windows. The car had Arizona license plates, and it was being groomed by a man in uniform whom I recognized from movies as a chauffeur.

Through Rockcliffe's open front door, I saw twin suitcases in the hall, sleek leather ones the color of Father Doyle's greyhound.

"Monica has arrived to visit, Minette," Lucilla told me. "Such is fate. The gods have smiled on me. But I have no time for your lesson today. You may return next week," she concluded, dismissing me with a little wave of her hand. I was amazed at how quickly my world had gone flat.

By Monday, I was champing at the bit. Lucilla waved to me as I came up the drive. Nelson offered me his paw. It was just like old times again. I felt that I was home. In the drawing room, I shucked off my shorts and sneakers and draped myself in my costume. I put Schubert's opus 40 on the gramophone and cranked it up. The lawn was squishy and cool beneath my bare feet. I raised my arms and lost myself in the dance.

As I went into my final whirl, I saw a woman leaning in the drawing room's open door. A slender blond in a pale linen sheath dress, her eyes were hidden behind cat's eye sunglasses. The glamour queen was smoking a cigarette. I knew right away that the woman was Monica.

"Brava," she cried in a voice that tilted as if she'd just heard a good joke. "Brava! Say, isn't that one of the curtains from the hall landing?" She dropped her cigarette onto the lawn and stubbed it out with the toe of her high-heeled sandal. Her toes were painted the same shade of coral as her lipstick.

"Honestly, Mother," she said. "The stunts you dream up to keep yourself amused are something else."

The strains of Schubert had died away, and I could hear the scratch, scratch sound of the needle on the edge of the record.

"And you, babycake?" She said to me with a grin. "Who are you supposed to be?"

The dusty curtain was twisted around me from my final spin. When I went to get up, my toe caught in one of the lace roses and tipped me back in a kind of mock curtsey. Above me, Rockcliffe rose cold and distinguished, its tower pointing up to the sky.

Down on the street below Lucilla's gates, I could hear a car revving its engine, and the neighborhood kids calling to each other to come and play ball. Back at my house, it was nearly time for supper. My mother would be at our stove and wondering where I was. That was the world I lived in. But it seemed as foreign to me as this one had suddenly become.

"Speak up, Minette," the queen said. "Show Monica your mettle."

Still dizzy from my whirl, I had the funniest feeling that I was flying.

"Mary," I replied. "My name is Mary Blonski." But my words fluttered back at me like a torn-up ticket home.

DOLL CAKE

My friend Angie is Italian, and her family makes a big fuss over birthday celebrations, unlike mine who are happy to let things go with a cake from the A&P and a quart of Hood's vanilla ice cream. Angie's cakes were always spectacular, right from the first one I'd ever seen when I was invited to her seventh birthday party. *Seven* is called the Age of Reason in the Catholic Church. It's the year you are officially declared to know right from wrong. We'd celebrated together with our First Holy Communion, walking down the center aisle at Saint Margaret's Church in frilly white dresses and dainty net veils like tiny brides. From that time onward, Father Doyle warned us, there would be black marks on our souls if we ever told a lie. And those marks would stay with us forever, unless we confessed our sins to a priest.

Angie's cake that year was four layers high, each layer separated by pudding: Vanilla. Chocolate. Vanilla. Chocolate. That was the lineup. And dead center in the round cake was a doll, buried to the waist in our dessert.

In her honor, the doll had black hair just like Angie's and brown eyes that could open and close. The cake was frosted to look like the doll's skirt, in three shades of pink with frosting rosettes along its border, colored red, yellow, and blue. In squiggly green icing across the top of the skirt, someone had written, "Buon Compleanno, Angelina!"

To my mind, Italian birthday parties were unbeatable, and so when Angie invited me to go to her cousin's tenth, I said yes as fast as I could, hoping for another one of those cakes. My sister Molly was invited too because she was the same age as Angie's sister. Molly was hoping for the little round cookies called anginettes that were frosted on top and sprinkled with tiny candy dots. We were obsessed with Italian desserts and lived for the rare occasions when we could get them. Our grandmothers had a way with pies and potatoes, but the gene necessary for creating extravagant cakes seemed to have passed them by.

"Hop in back, kids," said Mr. Gugliardi, holding open the door of his white Cadillac. Our destination was Town Plot, high on the west side of town. It was the land of grape arbors and manicured green lawns, little stone outdoor fireplaces, and of course, the magical cakes.

Our route took us down Willow Street, past four funeral parlors, three barbershops, and when we turned right at the traffic light, my favorite sight of all. In the third-floor window of a tall apartment building, and always in the same position as far as I could determine, was a monkey. It was either stuffed or tranquilized, its tail hooked over the curtain rod as it observed the traffic below. As often as I asked my father why there was a monkey in the window, he'd give me the same answer, in a tone of disgust.

"Who the hell knows?"

But Mr. Gugliardi had a different take on the situation.

"Maybe the guy who lives there is an organ grinder," he said.

The front seat conversation that day between Angie's parents centered on the gift they were bringing for Angie's cousin. Mrs. Gugliardi was excited about her choice.

She'd begun an "Add a Pearl" necklace when Connie was born, and she sat clutching this year's addition in its brightly wrapped gift box, expectant as one of the Magi on the way to visit the Child Jesus.

The way this particular necklace worked was swell. For twenty-four ninety-five plus tax, anyone could go to Clayton's Jewelry store on Bank Street and buy a thin gold chain with one starter pearl. The chain was fourteen carat, and the pearl was centered equidistant from the two sides of the clasp.

The beauty of "Add a Pearl" was twofold. As Mrs. Gugliardi had explained it to us, when you'd completed the strand you'd have a genuine pearl necklace to wear for high school graduation, or maybe even at your wedding. But because the giver had bought it one pearl at a time for the nominal sum of nine ninety-five, the gift wouldn't send her to the poor house.

"I just hope she appreciates it," Mrs. Gugliardi murmured.

When we got to Connie's house, we parked in front and walked up the driveway. The party was already underway. The guests had all brought their own lawn chairs, and a galvanized metal washtub filled with ice and bottles of multicolored Paul's sodas was set in the shade by the back porch steps.

The family's cars had been moved out of their garage and parked at the end of the street. Inside the garage were two long folding tables set up with folding chairs down both sides. The tables were spread with paper tablecloths printed in a design of party hats and streamers.

In Waterbury, at least among the folks lucky enough to have them, garage parties were common, because having parties in them kept the house clean. The tables in Connie's garage were spread with hard rolls and cold cuts and salads. When it was time to eat, the women of the family would go into the house and carry out the lasagnas and other hot dishes.

"Look," said Molly, nudging me. "At the end of the table. Anginettes!"

"Come sit on my swings," said Connie's sister, taking Molly by the hand. Angie got us each an orange soda and we looked around. Connie's parents lived on the second floor of the big two-family, so you had to climb the stairs to use the bathroom. It was through the kitchen, down the hall, and beyond the little bedroom Connie called hers.

When we went into her house, the first thing I saw was the cake, centered on the red Formica kitchen table. And it was a doll cake. Somehow Connie's mother had managed to make one twice the usual size, with a bigger doll than usual stuck in the middle of its yellow skirt.

I could hardly wait, but I knew the drill. At these parties, the cake did not come out until all the presents had been opened. And that did not take place until all the grown-ups had eaten their fill.

Because birthdays were special occasions, someone would always bring along a jug of his homemade wine, pressed from grapes in his own backyard arbor. He'd pour a shot into everyone's little paper cup and the toasting would begin.

"A salute!" they'd shout, kissing each other, the men as well as the women, in a way my Irish family would have found embarrassing.

"Papa! It's good!" Connie's relatives yelled to the tiny gray-haired winemaker sitting beside his black-clad wife. I could hear them through the open window of her bedroom.

"Look," said Angie. She was holding a satin jewelry case that she'd taken from the top of Connie's dresser. It was a round case the color of a robin's egg, with little flowers in the weave if you held it up to the light the right way.

"Let's open it," she said. "I bet the necklace is inside."

Angie set it on the bed and slid its zipper back. The whole top came away except for the part where the zipper was attached. Inside it lay the "Add a Pearl" necklace, coiled like a little snake in its soft blue nest.

"How do you think I'd look in pearls?" asked Angie. When she held the necklace up to her in the mirror, the chain came apart in her hands.

"I hardly touched it," she whispered. "This thing is about as strong as a cobweb."

"What are you going to do now?" I whispered back. I felt the same fear I had when I was in kindergarten and climbed to the top of the big girls' slide and realized I'd gone too high. All the rungs behind me that day were filled with girls waiting their turn, and my only way out was down. Even now, I remembered how all the sound seemed to die away and the moment got big and slow.

"You'll have to tell that you broke it," I said, glad that it wasn't me who had touched the necklace.

"What are you, crazy? My mother will kill me. We'll zip the case back up and get out of here."

"You came back just in time, girls," called Mrs. Gugliardi. "Connie is opening her gifts."

The presents had been stacked in the center of the big table and Connie opened them one by one. Angie and I hung back by the track that raises the garage doors up over your head and watched. There was a Madame Alexander doll dressed in a red cape like Little Red Riding Hood. I'd seen it in the Howland-Hughes toy department and admired it myself. Next came a game of Bingo, then a one-thousand-piece puzzle of Mount Rushmore, a pencil box, and a plaid dress.

"For back to school," her aunt explained. Connie made a face and everyone laughed.

"Saving the best for last?" Mr. Gugliardi joked, pointing to their gift with its blue butterfly wrapping paper. Connie opened the box and passed the pearl around on its velvet pad.

"Oh," said everyone. "Nice."

"Go inside and get your necklace, cara," Connie's mother told her. "Let everyone see how pretty it looks on you."

"You'll wear it to dance at your wedding," called an uncle who'd clearly had more than one paper cup of homemade wine. Connie came down the back stairs with her jewelry case in her hands. Angie and I exchanged glances.

"Shut up," she mouthed and looked away. But I could not stop watching.

Mrs. Gugliardi leaned forward in her lawn chair in anticipation. Alone on its black velvet background the little boxed pearl did not look like much, but set against the other nine already on the chain, you'd be able to get a good idea of how the necklace would look when it was completed. As Connie lifted it out, you could see the two sides of the chain separate. The pearls were clustered together on the long side, hanging on like passengers going down on the Titanic.

"Merda!" screamed Mrs. Gugliardi. "It's broken!"

"Well, I didn't do it." Connie's lower lip was pushing out in what my mother would have called a pout, a facial expression forbidden at our house. Connie stood motionless, waiting for whatever would come next.

"Are you sure?" her mother asked. "How else could this have happened?"

"It was like that when I opened the case. I never touched the dumb old thing. I don't even like it, anyway."

Connie's voice was shaky. The way everyone was looking at her, I was not surprised. Mrs. Gugliardi's lips were pressed tightly together, but her eyes flashed sparks in the light from the garage's overhead light bulb. It was a face that my father would have described as her "slapping face." My mother had the same look herself, sometimes, and I did all I could to avoid it.

"We'll talk about this some more at bedtime," Connie's mother told her. "Maybe by then you'll remember what happened if I give you time to think about it." Putting the new pearl into the blue case with the necklace, she looked apologetically at Mrs. Gugliardi, then changed the subject.

"Anyway," she told Connie, "it's time now for your birthday cake."

Her grandmother lit the candles on the doll's skirt, ten of them plus one for luck, and we all sang "Happy Birthday." When Connie cut the cake, sure enough it was my favorite kind, with the pudding filling. Someone passed me a piece, and it was one with a big blue frosting flower on it. But the weird thing was that I couldn't seem to swallow it. I put my napkin over the plate so no one would see and slipped it into the trash bag by the door.

"You eat fast," someone teased me. "You want another slice?"

Mrs. Gugliardi gave us the high sign, and we left right after that. As soon as his Caddy rounded the corner, Mrs. Gugliardi let loose.

"Madonna mia," she began. Her voice sounded hard enough to write her name on glass. "You can't give anything nice to some people. I should have known. That brat's party was just like in the Bible. I cast my pearls before swine."

"You're right, baby." Mr. Gugliardi extended his left arm out the car window in a circular gesture that indicated he was making a right turn.

"Hey, don't you criticize my family," she snapped. In a lower tone, like a boiling pot that had been turned down to a long, slow simmer, she added, "That kid would have been smiling out of the other side of her face if she was mine. I'd have knocked her into the middle of next week."

"Cosi va il mondo, baby. That's life," said Mr. Gugliardi, pulling up in front of our house.

My sister squeezed my hand, happy that she'd gone to the party. Angie sat with her face toward the window, stiff and still as the monkey down on West Main Street. When we got out of the car, she didn't even turn to say good-bye. I wondered what Father Doyle would have said about the day's events. Telling on Angie would be like putting her neck on the chopping block. But unless she confessed, the necklace would remain a black spot on Angie's soul.

It was lucky for us, I thought, that eternity was still a long way off. So surely there would be time for Angie to fix things. As for myself, I was over my craving for doll cake. I hoped I'd never see another one again.

GLADS

Gladioli are also known as the sword lily, and when you see a whole field of them, you can understand why. The flowers stood in formation as upright as fixed bayonets on the evening my father took my sister and me to buy some for our mother. We were buying them because Mom was on the warpath. And so we set out after supper in Dad's baby blue Ford to get what my father termed a peace offering. If the flowers had the effect he was hoping for, the rest of our night would be spent in peace.

The gladioli farm was north of us on Thomaston Avenue, a curving road bounded on the west by the Naugatuck River and train tracks that could take a person south all the way to New York City. The farm was actually a long field that stretched along the east side of Thomaston Avenue, with a tiny house at one end of it. As for the rest, it was flowers as far as our eyes could see.

The glads were planted in rows according to color: red, pink, salmon, purple, yellow, white. Some were already harvested and their cut ends placed into galvanized buckets awaiting buyers. Those bouquets were in bunches of a single color. But Dad, fearing to choose a color my mother might find irritating, asked the farmer to make up a fresh bouquet with a few of every color he had.

"Well, kids, your mother is as cranked up as the Mad Bomber tonight. But these should do the trick to defuse her."

The Mad Bomber was, we knew, a mysterious madman whose diabolical plan was to blow up Gotham City a little at a time. We also knew, from reading Batman comic books, that Gotham was another name for New York City. Mom and Grandma had taken us there once, on a silver train that left from the enormous brick station on Meadow Street. I'd never forgotten the wild-eyed man in front of Radio City Music Hall with his sign that read, "Repent. The end is near." I had worried that the Mad Bomber might come to our end of town on Willow Street, but Dad had told me to relax.

"Blowing up Waterbury would be small potatoes for him compared with Manhattan," he'd said.

The farmer was standing next to his Flowers for Sale sign, dressed in a khaki shirt and workpants. It looked as if he was out of hearing range, and if he had overheard my father's reference to Mom's mood, he gave no sign of it. I looked down into the gladioli's little faces. Their edges were ruffled like the hem of my First Holy Communion dress, their centers hidden inside their closely packed, funnel shaped blooms that sprang from both sides of the flower stalks like buttons on a clarinet.

"Are we in the country?" asked my sister Molly.

"Not hardly," said the farmer. But Molly remained skeptical. Although it had taken us less than fifteen minutes to get here from our house, the contrast between our cement sidewalks and the color-packed field was startling. That such different kinds of places could exist at the same time, and practically around the corner, was an amazing piece of information. And the way we had moved from one reality to another simply by changing location, in our case by a short trip north in Dad's car, made it even better. I wondered if my mother knew about this. If so, then perhaps it was the reason why she had begun to take driving lessons from the E-Z Learn Driving School every Wednesday afternoon.

Her lessons had begun right around the time Molly was gone all day at school. My father liked our mother at home, even if there was nothing much for her to do. But it had become apparent to all of us that Mom did not feel the same about the situation.

We stood together in the late afternoon light of August, a light that was not quite sunset and still a long way away from being dark. We were quiet, each of us, my father, Molly, the farmer, and I, lost in our own thoughts, admiring the flowers. Dad took a Kool cigarette from the pack he had stowed in the rolled-up sleeve of his white T-shirt. He offered one to the farmer and lit them both. We could see that Dad was not ready to get back into the car yet and go home.

By now, our mother would have the supper dishes washed and put away, perhaps slamming the cupboard doors, boiling over what it was that had set her off. Sometimes the reason for her mood was a mystery to us, but this time, the reason was a remark that we had all heard for ourselves. Grandma's brother Lamar had come to visit, and on his way upstairs, when he'd greeted Mom he'd added, "I wonder what you do with yourself all day just hanging around the house."

"He should have quit while he was ahead," Dad mused. "'Hello' would have done just fine."

My great uncle's comment had opened the floodgates to Mom's frequent dissertations on her latest idea, namely that we should move to a different house, one that was all our own, minus Dad's parents and their busybody company.

"Maybe Mom will forget by the time we get back," Molly offered.

"Don't get your hopes up," Dad replied, lighting a new cigarette from the glowing tip of his old one.

The gladioli farmer cleared his throat and began to talk.

"These flowers here are a lot of work," he began. "You've got the corms to dig up each fall. The bulbs, that is. And you've got to store them where they will dry. When you dig them up you've got to trim their tops and take off the old corms, then put them down to rest. I use my cellar to store them through the winter so they can't freeze."

Surely the man must have seen that we were not the type of folks to go to such great lengths for flowers, but he went on, capping the recital of his flower-growing toils with a statement that sounded like a fairy tale.

"Hummingbirds love them," he added, gesturing toward the glads. "They like to drink the nectar in their little cups."

In the future, Molly and I would learn about hummingbirds from a series of trading cards that came as prizes inside the boxes of Grandma's Tetley teabags. But on that night, the idea of birds that hummed and drank from flower cups was so fantastic that it gave us hope that anything was possible in our world. Molly's eyes glowed as she asked, "Can I see one? A humming bird, I mean."

"It's the wrong time of day for that, honey," said the farmer. "But come again some morning, and we'll give it a try."

Unlike the sweet smelling lavender colored blossoms on the lilac tree in our backyard, the gladioli flowers had no fragrance that I could detect. They were about show, I surmised, rather than perfume. I looked at Dad and wondered if he was thinking about being back in our kitchen, settling into the platform rocker by the big double windows, pouring himself a cup of coffee and working the daily word jumble puzzle in the evening *Waterbury American.*

The field of bright, spiky flowers stood perfectly still in the slight breeze as the farmer rattled off the names of his charges in a foreign language that I would discover, when I started high school, was Latin.

"Childsii. Lemoinei. Nanceianus. Groff." His words sounded to me like the incantation for a magic spell, but it seemed to wake Dad out of his trance. Suddenly, he was restless to be off.

"You know about the language of flowers?" the man asked us, as Dad fished the Ford's ignition key out of the pocket of his chino trousers.

"All the flowers mean something. Iris, for example, means fidelity. The lily of the valley? Happiness. But these here glads, what they mean with all those blossoms on each and every stalk? Well, they mean generosity. Come again, folks. Any time."

Molly climbed in back as Dad held the car door open for her. I sat in front, and the farmer placed our bouquet in my arms. We turned in our seats to look back at him growing smaller and smaller, waving good-bye with the field behind him as we headed home.

"Do you think our flowers are magic?" asked Molly. I was wondering the same thing myself. If so, would their magic work even if the recipient was unaware of the flower's secret meaning? Part of the gladioli's generosity was that they'd last at least a week in fresh water. Perhaps their seven-day gift would infuse our house with its promise.

I held the bouquet carefully across my lap, despite the fact that their wet ends were trickling water down my legs and into my socks. Their potential far outweighed a minor discomfort. The idea that the flowers, like the divine intervention we often heard about at Sunday Mass, might cheer my mother up and calm her down began to work its magic on me too. I relaxed my death grip on the flowers and took a deep breath of the air rushing in through the car's open windows. I let it blow my hair around even though it would be a mess by the time we got home.

"Maybe we'll get the cats and sit on the front porch," Molly said. "We can watch the cars go up and down Willow Street and pick out the ones we like best."

I knew that the increasingly busy street was another of my mother's pet peeves. Many of our old neighbors were moving away to other parts of town. It felt sad to say good-bye over and over and to feel that we were being left behind.

"Maybe Mom and Dad and our grandparents will come and sit with us," I replied. I liked the nights when we all sat on the porch with the long summer day behind us and almost ready for sleep. Our mother was restless for change. But Molly and I liked things the way they were. I had the idea that Dad did too.

How beautiful the stiff, proud flowers looked in my lap, their colors lined up together like a rainbow.

"Mom will be happy again when she sees these," I said.

"Maybe so," Dad replied, taking his foot off the gas pedal to slow us to a crawl. Lighting another cigarette with the lighter from the dashboard, he added,

"Well, kids, we'll find out soon enough."

VANITY

The year that I took ballroom-dancing lessons, I was chubby and shy, with myopic blue eyes and fine, frizzy hair. I longed to be beautiful, and my vanity table led me to believe that it might one day be possible. My parents had given me the vanity at Christmas. It stood waiting for me beneath our tree, a big red bow on its rosette bordered mirror, when I woke up that morning.

The table had been ordered from the Sears Catalogue's unpainted furniture section and its top sanded and varnished to blond sleekness by my father in his basement workshop, a place he'd laughingly put off-limits for the month of December as Santa Land. My parents had also provided a brass stool for it, one with a heart-shaped back.

Seated before my vanity on its white velvet cushion, I leaned forward and peered into the mirror. My reflection swam up at me from the depths of the silver lake. I could see my breath on the glass, the invisible made real. Clearly this was a setting where magic could occur. My vanity, I saw, would go forward with me in time, reflecting all the things I could and would become.

My twin bed with its heart-shaped headboard stood opposite from where I placed the vanity. And at night, lying beneath my comforter, I imagined I was cocooned, a moth in its chrysalis that would emerge one day as a butterfly.

None of the doors in our house had locks, and so the vanity's secret drawer was my retreat. Its kidney-shaped table had little wooden side arms that swung out to reveal the single drawer with a tiny wooden knob. The vanity's skirt completely encircled the table, and what a skirt it was. In three long tiers of ruffled white organza, its skirt was part ballerina tutu and part wedding gown. It was like the dress Cinderella wore to the ball where she met her prince. It was like the robes angels in pictures wore as they floated to heaven.

I arranged my mirror, comb, and brush set on its top, set at an angle the way it was shown on the lid of the box it had come in. The set was Grandma's Christmas gift to me, and its gold mirror was the trio's star, embossed on its back with wreaths of tiny flowers. There was a matching comb with little plastic teeth that raked my hair like fingers, and a nylon brush that was too soft to combat my hair's winter static electricity. That was something I'd already noticed about beautiful things. They frequently proved better to look at than to use.

My mother contributed a boudoir lamp, its lacy shade tied with a satin bow. All that was left to complete the picture was for me to fill my secret drawer. The first thing that went in was my Revlon Pretty in Pink lipstick. Next, a Pond's compact, its powder a pale shade that made the fuzz in my cheeks stand out when I rubbed it the wrong way.

My mother's bureau produced a round brass pillbox with a red jewel that gleamed like an idol's eye, and from Grandma's dresser, a tiny blue-glass purse-sized perfume bottle with a little funnel for filling it. I added the miniature plaster monkeys Dad had won at Savin Rock because I liked their little scrunched up, grinning faces that illustrated the old adage of "See, hear, and speak no evil."

For jewelry, I had a simulated pearl necklace and matching bracelet and my Miraculous Medal brooch set with tiny blue rhinestones. My vanity drawer winked up at me like Ali Baba's cave, an "open sesame" of talismans. I wished I had a love letter to top things off, tied with a blue ribbon.

Down in the cellar, in a box of old books, I came upon my father's grammar school autograph book. Someone named Yolanda had written, "You have big ideas, and don't I know it." I liked the sound of it, and so I copied the message out onto a sheet of writing paper and signed it with the name of the dark-haired boy who worked at the corner grocery. Although he did not know it, he was my secret crush.

Traffic in the part of the city rolled relentlessly up and down Willow Street. Neighbors quarreled with each other from their back porches. Dogs howled at the moon from the ends of their chains. But in my bedroom, there was order. My vanity became my altar. I applied my lipstick and powder with care, hoping for a miracle like the one Father Malloy performed each Sunday at Mass, changing water into wine.

I guess my mother noticed a change in me, because she came into my room one night to tell me she had signed me up for dancing school. Mom had paid in advance, and I knew it would be impossible to tell her that the idea terrified me.

"Good thing you took that charm class at the Girls' Club," she continued. "If you're worried about what to do, you can check your manual."

That was the pink-covered book called *White Gloves and Party Manners.* Under subsection three, I'd learned that boys like girls who are the following:

1. Fun to be with
2. Easy to talk to
3. Good listeners
4. Good sports

The manual concluded its pep talk with a breezy admonition: "So relax! And be yourself!" This seemed to me to be a complete contradiction for someone as self-conscious as I was. But I thought it over anyway.

The Mrs. Majetski School of Dancing met on Friday evenings in the Women's Club Hall, with music provided by her daughter, determinedly pounding on an upright piano and perhaps hoping, by sheer volume, to sound like an orchestra. The boys lined up against one wall, the girls against another. Despite the wintergreen lifesaver I'd chewed to sweeten my breath, I could taste my fear.

I felt as stiff as my plaid taffeta dress, its full skirt fluffed out with two crinoline slips. My first pair of nylon stockings was held up by a garter belt, and despite my best efforts, their seams were as wavy as the squiggles on a Hostess cupcake. I was wearing a bra, not that I needed one, and a headband to hold my hair in place. In fact, I had on so much equipment that I felt like a knight in armor. But when the boys charged across the hall to ask the girls to dance, I had no lance for jousting.

My first partner's head came up to my bosom, just at the level of the velvet bow that marked my dress's waist.

"Do you like school?" I asked, attempting to be "easy to talk to."

"Are you nuts?"

I laughed then, shooting for "fun to be with."

I looked down into my partner's crew cut. It looked like pale stubs of cut wheat. I glanced sideways at my Timex watch on the wrist that clutched his shoulder. In forty-five more minutes, I could go home.

On the far side of the room, I saw Chet, the boy from the corner market who was my secret crush. He was fox trotting with a girl who lived one street over from my house. How easily his hand rested on her tiny waist. Her hair lay on her shoulders in a smooth pageboy. Her circle skirt swayed when he raised her arm to twirl her.

If you were going to be popular at dancing school, it started on the first night with an invitation to walk down to Pickett's Drugstore for a Coke after dancing. I waited alone on the front steps of the Women's Club for my father to pick me up.

"Your chauffeur is here," Dad said. Then to cheer me up, he added, "We'll stop by the bakery for doughnuts on the way home."

The bakery was in the Brooklyn section of town, on John Street. On Friday nights, the storefront was closed, so patrons walked down the alley into the warm back room where bakers in white clothes shoveled rye bread into the ovens using long wooden paddles.

Dad had gone to grammar school with one of the bakers, and if it was a slow night, he'd let me squirt red jelly into the fresh doughnuts using a machine with a pointed spout. The baker rolled his eyes at Dad when he saw me all dressed up.

"If only I was young again," he laughed.

I traced my name in flour on the counter while Dad counted out the change. I tried to think positive thoughts. *Maybe I appeal to older men*, I told myself. When we got home, I ate three jelly doughnuts in ten minutes.

"Good thing I bought a dozen," Dad said.

I put on my flannel nightgown and went to bed. Outside my window, on the back porch railing, I could see my cat, her fur puffed up like a muff. Sometimes I'd open the window and bring her into bed with me. In cold weather, her fur was as silky as Grandma's mink stole. Priscilla did not look like the same cat who stayed out all night in the spring yowling at the neighbor's tom until my mother grabbed her and shut her in the cellar.

But my mother was wasting her time as far as I was concerned. I already knew the score. It was why I practiced kissing my reflection in the mirror after I applied my Pretty in Pink lipstick. It was Julie London singing "Fever" on the *Ed Sullivan Show* and the red nylon baby doll pajamas the newly married woman next door hung out on her clothesline. It culminated in a baby like the one my cousin Madeline had in her stomach when she'd come by at Christmas to see our tree.

"Procreation," I whispered, trying on for size the word I'd discovered in *The Catholic Transcript*. It had a grandeur about it that dignified what seemed to me a potentially awkward and embarrassing process.

The next thing that happened was that I got my first pair of eyeglasses. It was amazing how much I could see. You'd have guessed that I'd be happy about it, but twenty-twenty vision proved to be a mixed blessing. For starters, my mother told the optometrist that price was a consideration, and so my frame selection was limited to the glasses in the tray of his second drawer. The blue and white harlequin plastic frames she chose swept up at the corners "like cat's eyes," Mom said, hoping to encourage me.

"Beauty is in the eye of the beholder," she added in a tone that left no room for argument. But that was exactly the problem. Now that my fuzzy focus had been sharpened, I was "before" in the "before and after" pictures in *Redbook* magazine. I was so unnerved by this that I ate a whole bag of Hershey's Kisses.

After dinner, I went up to the corner store and bought a comic book. I chose the classic comic version of *Midsummer Night's Dream* by William Shakespeare. I thought it might be comforting to read a story about people with donkeys' heads falling in love anyway. Chet was working the counter register.

"Wow!" he said, ringing up my purchase. "You must be an intellectual."

"I saw you at dancing school last Friday," I told him.

"My mother made me go."

"Mine too," I told him. He handed me my change. I was so rocked by our conversation that when I got home, I checked my mirror to see if I looked different.

That Friday, Chet asked me to rumba to "Hernando's Hideaway," in spite of my new glasses.

"Dancing class is almost over," he said.

Mrs. Majetski had planned a Valentine's Day theme for our dancing debut at the end of the session. Our parents were invited to watch us practice our accomplishments, and what to wear to the ball was the main topic of conversation in the ladies' room of the Women's Club. My grandmother decided that I should have a gown made for the occasion.

"Something youthful," my mother said.

"Something grand," Grandma countered. And so the three of us paid a visit to Madame Zarovka, a Russian expatriate who made dresses. The sign on the door of her store on Prospect Street was spelled shoppe. And her dresses were called creations. When she produced the bolt of white chiffon, I was in heaven. The billowing fabric was just like my vanity skirt.

"Can I have ruffles?" I asked.

"No," said Madame Zarovka, looking at my stomach. "For you, we drape."

I lobbied to have my gown be strapless, but my mother said no.

"Modesty is important."

"Okay," Madame Zarovka replied, coaxing a fold of chiffon across my shoulder. "We do detachable sleeves. Like so."

"But all this white," my mother complained, her eyes raking the bolts of fabric for an addition.

Pushing back a strand of hair that had escaped from the braids coiled over her ears, Madame Zarovka thought for a moment, then said the magic word.

"Sashes!"

"Yes," my mother agreed. "We can do them like the queen's, draping from one shoulder."

"Maybe a red one, for Valentine's Day. And a green one, for Christmas," Grandma said. "And a purple sash too, that ties in back in a big bow."

I took off my glasses and held my breath while Madame Zarovka pinned and draped the chiffon. I thought about the heart-shaped locket I'd bought at Woolworth's and my white gloves with the little seed pearls sewn on their cuffs. That night, I wrote in my diary, "My gown for the Valentine's dance is exquisite. In it, I will be transformed."

The entry, recorded in peacock blue ink, looked so impressive that it was worth having to get out the dictionary to look up the spelling of "exquisite." Outside the window, snow was falling, white as chiffon under the streetlight. I lulled myself to sleep, reciting the names of my mother's perfumes: Emeraude, Blue Grass, Desert Flower.

"I can always count on you to run to the store for me," my mother said, handing me money for a pound of ground beef. Little did she know the reason I so eagerly agreed.

"See you Friday," Chet said, handing me my bag. He made a dancing motion with his hands and hips.

My completed gown hung on the bedroom door beneath a plastic cover. I sat at my vanity and combed out my hair. Grandma had set it in three tight rows of pin curls, and I had more waves than I knew what to do with. The more I combed, the more my hair stuck out.

"Close your eyes," my mother said. "A good squirt of Aqua Net will fix this."

I got into my white dress, my white satin shoes, and applied my lipstick. My cheeks were pink from excitement, and my eyes looked extra blue. It seemed as if magic might really happen that night in my bedroom in my new gown.

"Hold on a minute," my mother said. "We need to snap on the sleeves."

"And the red sash," Grandma added. "I'll hook it on for you."

It was amazing how something that had started out so right could suddenly go so wrong. My gauzy chiffon strapless gown had turned into swaddling clothes. And the red sash, running from north to south across my chest, looked liked an illustration for the temperate zone in my geography book.

"Now for your glasses," Mom said, handing them to me. "And don't forget to smile."

I stayed in the bathroom of the Women's Club as long as I could, watching the other girls primp. Some of them looked worse than I did. But some of them looked a whole lot better.

When I heard Mrs. Majetski's daughter strike up the "Grand March" on the piano, there was nothing else for it but to join the dance.

The balcony was crowded with parents watching their children. Cries of "Hey, look over here!" rang out as the fathers snapped photos. Flashbulbs were going off all over the place. I saw spots before my eyes as I danced by with a tall boy wearing white bucks.

"Don't step on my shoes," he warned me.

"Don't worry," I replied. "I'll keep as far away from you as possible."

My mother waved her handkerchief to get my attention. I lowered my eyes and focused on my partner's tie. It was a red tie, and it dawned on me that of the thirty boys on the dance floor, nearly everyone's tie was red. My father was no doubt in the balcony making a crack about a red-tie sale in Waterbury. It made me laugh, in spite of myself.

"What's so funny?" my partner asked. When I told him, he laughed too.

The next number was the fox trot. My partner was the crew cut boy from the first night's dance.

"Step. Close. Step. And one," he counted, his face sweaty with effort. No one mentioned my sash to me, and I was grateful.

At nine o'clock, Mrs. Majetski stopped the music.

"Bravo! Brava! Brave!" she called, clapping her hands. The parents all joined in. Taking advantage of their enthusiasm, she continued, "Mothers and fathers, don't forget! My next session starts in two weeks."

My mother and I waited on the sidewalk for Dad to bring the car. Chet walked by us with the girl from one street over.

"Isn't that the boy from the corner store?" my mother asked.

"Uh huh," I replied, feigning indifference. I'd sucked my breath in a little too much while Madame Zarovka was draping me, and my dress was digging into my waist something fierce. My white shoes slipped a bit on the icy curb as I climbed into the car's backseat.

"That was some ball, Cinderella," said my father.

"It made me wish I was twelve again," my mother replied. "I think we should sign her up for the next session."

When I got home, I took off my gown and put it in the closet. I put away my shoes and gloves, but I kept my locket on. I didn't go near my vanity. I didn't want to face myself in its mirror.

Safe in the dark, I allowed myself to think about the dance. In the Women's Club ladies' room, I'd imagined I might have a good cry when it was over. But now it didn't seem to matter as much. From my bed, I studied the ruffles on my vanity skirt. I remembered the silly letter I'd copied for my secret drawer and got out of bed to tear it up.

"It's not your fault," I told my vanity, remembering that for at least a while, in my bedroom, I had been transformed. And if it had happened once, I told myself, there was a chance that it might happen again. When I got back into bed, I pulled my covers up over me like a cocoon.

ADVANTAGE

An August hotter than Lily could ever have imagined began with too much water. When the flood waters roared down from Winsted to Waterbury, the city was cut in half from east to west. The Naugatuck River was so wide at its crest that the separate sides of the city seemed like islands to observers gathered on their respective banks. Boats motored along Main Street. Rowboats tied up to the second-floor porches of houses. These sights were so bizarre that the flood seemed like a very bad dream.

The night before, Lily and her family had gathered on the front lawn of their house to watch hurricane Diana's tail winds blow across the sky, forcing the limbs of the elms and maples to bow down before her. The yellow lights of their house behind them seemed nearly extinguished by the force of the storm.

Next morning, there was not a drop of water when Lily turned the bathroom faucet on. The toilet's water tank emptied with a deep, moaning sound and refused to refill. The radio announcer on their tiny transistor radio called it Black Friday 1955 in Connecticut. The flood was a natural disaster.

The Red Cross set up at the State Armory for flood relief. Waterburians were advised to report there for typhoid vaccinations. Lily stood with her family in a line that snaked back on itself up Field Street to Grand so far that she could not see its end. Above her head, helicopters beat through the sky, bringing supplies across the water to the hospital on the far banks of the river.

That night, Lily ran a fever from the typhoid shot. Her left arm swelled up and grew hard. When she closed her eyes to stop the room from spinning, she imagined she saw houses being carried down the river like toys.

"Lily is delirious," she heard her mother say. "This city is no place for a child right now." When Lily woke the next morning, her fever had broken, and her mother told her she was going to the country for a few days. Country to them meant Plymouth, the town where their cousin Roland lived. They only saw Roland at the annual family picnic he liked to host each summer, and so they had been surprised when he phoned to offer them his home until the city returned to normal.

"Lucky for us, the phone still works," Lily's mother said.

Lily was used to city streets and found the winding back roads a wilderness of green.

"How do people here find their way?" she'd asked her father.

"Probably they drop a trail of breadcrumbs," he'd joked. But his allusion to Hansel and Gretel on their way to the witch's house had only increased Lily's sense of unease. Lily's big worry was Roland's daughter Heidi, with her long brown braids and slightly crossed brown eyes. Unhampered by daily baths, her up-close scent was metallic, and her off-focus stare was bold.

Lily's mother laid Heidi's boldness at the door of her mother. As slender as the cigarettes she chain-smoked between her Light My Fire lipsticked lips, Roland's wife, Magda, was as different from Lily's mother as a timber wolf was from Lassie. The factory where Magda worked had made her common, Lily's mother said, smoothing her white apron over her starched cotton housedress.

"Remember that Heidi has not had your advantages," Lily's mother told her, meaning Catholic school with its focus on good behavior.

The year before, Heidi, who was four years older than Lily, had taken her into her parents' bedroom while Roland's annual picnic was at its height. The blond wood headboard of their bedroom set had sliding panels at its back that opened to reveal compartments that made Lily think of tiny, secret rooms.

"Look," Heidi had said, removing a hardcover book with a dark cover. *Guide to Marital Relations* was its title. Next to it in the compartment were sealed foil packets of what felt like rings.

"Open one," Heidi had urged. Lily removed a white rubber case like the one the butcher at the meat market filled to make sausage.

"It's a rubber," Heidi explained. "It tells all about them in the *Guide*." There were no pictures in the guidebook, only words. In tiny print, Lily read about the fertilization process of eggs.

"Take the domestic fowl," page twenty-five began.

"Better put the book back," Heidi whispered. "I think that someone's coming."

Lily packed her own suitcase for her trip to the country. She decided to include her Ginny doll for company, and placed the little doll's green straw hat on her head.

"Good-bye. Have fun," called her mother as her father backed their car down Roland's narrow drive.

"My mom's at work," Heidi said, pushing Lily's suitcase to one side of the hall with her foot. "So this is a good time for us to go look in her bedroom." She rummaged in the closet, tossing skirts and dresses onto the unmade bed.

"What do you think of this on me?" she asked, pirouetting in Magda's Hawaiian blouse with the bright yellow pineapple print.

Heidi's grandmother was in the backyard, hanging out wash. Her mouth was filled with wooden clothespins that looked like little tusks. Her white hair was pinned up on top of her head in a knot.

"We're going to pick blueberries, Oma," Heidi called to her. "Okay to take these cans?"

She handed Lily one of the coffee cans she'd taken from Roland's workbench. He used them to hold all the different-sized nails that Heidi had just emptied out onto the driveway. The dark berries grew on a steep bank behind Roland's ranch house. The underbrush was thick with bees and full of thorns. Grasshoppers jumped ahead of them in droves. They seemed to Lily like friendly little scouts showing her the way to the ripe fruit. Roland's yard ended in a cliff with a view of the valley below his house. Even though Lily knew what to expect, it was still a thrill to look down at the Pleasant Valley Drive-in Movie Theater and its big outdoor screen.

If you'd gone there at dusk before the mosquitoes had begun to bite, you could watch the movie story play out. The novelty of it made up for not being able to hear the words. But Lily found it scary to be so close to the edge. Looking down at the valley below so far away and silent reminded her of the sermon where Satan takes Jesus up to a mountain to show him everything that could be his if he'd just do what the devil wanted.

"Chicken skin," said Heidi, coming up next to Lily and pinching the little hairs her thoughts had raised on her arms.

"Girls! Girls! Come back!" Heidi's grandmother called in her soft German accent. Her voice was seconded by Roland's angry yell.

"I'm gonna catch it," Heidi said, scratching the mosquito bites on one leg with the sole of her shoe.

"Why?" Lily asked. "What do you think you did wrong?"

"Who knows? Since when do they need excuses?"

In their knotty pine-paneled kitchen, Magda sat smoking, tapping her narrow foot in its black high-heeled sandal. Cards were laid out on the table for their nightly pinochle game. Heidi's grandmother was making sandwiches for supper. A loaf of Reymond's white bread was on the counter next to a stack of greasy salami slices.

"Margarine, Lily?" she asked.

"No, thank you. I like butter."

"She's too good for us, Roland. Just like her mother," Magda said.

"Lay off, Mag," answered Roland, taking off his work shirt. Lily could see his chest hair over the V of his undershirt. It looked like barbed wire.

"Where's Heidi?" he asked.

"She's in Dutch."

"For what?" Heidi peered in through the screen door.

"You left a bunch of nails in the driveway. I could have got a flat. You think money for new tires grows on trees?"

"We used the can for picking berries, Dad. I just didn't think."

"You never think. That's the problem," Roland told her.

"Jesus! You're wearing my new blouse!" Magda was on her feet, yanking Heidi by one arm around the door frame into the house.

"You little shit. I kick a press all day to buy nice things, and you do this?" she added, as the top button of the berry-stained blouse came open from her shaking.

"You deserve a beating. Roland?" Lily's cousin stood, sliding the belt out of his work pants. He advanced on Heidi, cracking the strap against his leg. She ran for the living room, her father close behind.

From the kitchen doorway, Lily watched as Heidi crawled beneath the coffee table, trying to hide. The table's top was mirrored in blue glass like the gazing ball in Lily's mother's garden. How far away her home seemed right now.

Roland's belt cracked, raising a cloud of dust from the sofa.

"Careful, Ro. Don't hurt the table," Magda called. Heidi's screams made Lily put her hands over her ears, but Heidi's grandmother kept making sandwiches as if nothing was wrong. Lily could see red stripe lines on Heidi's legs where they stuck out beneath the table. And beyond her, on the fireplace mantle, the stuffed wildcat Roland had shot in Maine looked down on them with its green glass eyes, its mouth fixed open in a snarl.

Next morning after cereal, the girls planned their day. Heidi's face was still puffy from crying, but she acted as if last night had been a scene on the drive-in movie screen and not worth discussing.

"What do you want to do, Lily?"

"I don't know. You pick."

Heidi brightened. "I'll show you something different."

Outside, the dew was still heavy on the unmowed lawn, and the sun caught it here and there in spangles. The grasshoppers lay on the long blades of grass, resting before beginning their busy day.

"It's easier to catch them when they are wet," Heidi advised, handing Lily an empty milk bottle. At its bottom, a pale residue of milk from the unwashed bottle slopped from side to side. The grasshoppers Heidi dropped in clung to the high part of the bottle to get away. Heidi led Lily around to the back of the house where a big brown spider had made a web by the back steps.

"Watch this," Heidi said. She took out a little green grasshopper and pulled off its back legs. The grasshopper worked its jaws, spitting up the brown liquid that Lily's father called tobacco juice. Heidi pitched it into the web. Lily screamed. How fast the spider moved. A bite, a silky weave to wrap his gift, then back to his corner to wait.

"Now you do one."

But Lily tipped the bottle over so the others could escape. The funny thing, though, was that the other grasshoppers were as hard to coax out of the bottle as they had been to put in. Lily clapped her hand on the bottom until it was empty. Heidi watched from the top step, chewing on her braid.

"Mom? Can I come home now?" Lily whispered into the kitchen phone. Heidi's grandmother's false teeth grinned at her from their container on the counter. It was labeled Chopper Hopper and shaped like a motorcycle.

"Not till Friday, Lily. You know that I don't drive. We'll come when your father gets out of work tomorrow night."

"Another day?" Lily's voice rose in a squeak.

"Make the best of it, honey. It's a lot cooler there than it is at home in Waterbury."

Lily hung up the phone carefully so it would not make a sound. Upstairs in Heidi's bedroom that she shared, her Ginny doll sat on the folding cot. Lily packed the doll's little cardboard suitcase and set it in her hand.

There was jelly roll for dessert after supper. Magda was in a good mood. She'd gotten a lot of overtime at the factory. Because of the flood, many of her coworkers had not been able to get to work.

"I'm on the right side of the river," she laughed, stubbing out her cigarette in her leftover cake.

"Me and Roland are going out tonight to celebrate," she continued. Lily knew that it was "Roland and I," but she also knew Magda would be angry if she told her so. Magda's eyes looked as shiny as melted caramels. Roland was smiling too. Heidi saw her opportunity and took it.

"It's so hot, Ma. Can we sleep in your room? Just for tonight?" Their room at the corner of the house had two windows as well as the house's only fan.

"Why not?" Magda told her. "Lily's going home tomorrow. Let's give her a good night's rest. She's probably sick of sleeping on that cot."

Lily knew that what Heidi really wanted was another crack at the *Guide*. They changed into the baby doll pajamas Magda had bought them. Lily's were green; Heidi's, blue. The pajamas had baggy pants like a baby's, with elastic gathers at the waist and legs. The tops were billowy, with elastic necks that you could push off your shoulders. They looked cool with the tiers of ruffles cascading down their fronts, but on a night as hot as this one, the nylon fabric made Lily feel as if she'd forgotten to towel off after a swim.

"Listen to this," Heidi said, reading paragraph on glands out loud. The *Guide* lay open on her pillow. Lily guessed it was Magda's side of the bed because of the makeup streaks on it. Heidi kicked the top sheet aside and settled in.

"I started my period last month," she continued. "Now I can have a baby. I bet you don't know how people get babies. Do you? But I do."

"Turn out the light, kids," called Roland. "Don't let me catch you awake when we get home."

It was hot in the bedroom, even with the light out and the fan on high. Heidi took off the top of her baby dolls.

"You too," she said. "It's cooler." Mounded together on the rug, their blue and green ruffles swayed in the fan's breeze like little waves. Lily drifted off to sleep, the sheet pulled to her chin. The alarm clock's luminous hands pointed to midnight when she woke. Heidi's hand was on her arm.

"Let's play a game," she whispered.

It was so quiet in the house. The only sound at all was the whirring of the fan blades.

"If you don't play, I'll tell everyone that you made me read the *Guide*," Heidi continued.

"But you were the one who wanted to read it. That book was your idea."

"Yeah, but I'll tell them it was you who snooped and found it."

Heidi's hand moved down to Lily's waist, stopping at the elastic on her Baby Doll bloomers.

"And you and I both know that if you tell your mother anything about the *Guide* or my game she'll kill you," Heidi continued. "She is such a holier-than-thou prude."

"This is what Magda and Roland do," Heidi said. "Shut up and you'll be okay."

The sheet tangled around Lily's ankles. She felt as if she was drowning. The whirring fan became the motor on the rescue party's boat, a boat that would not arrive in time to save her. Lily closed her eyes and floated out of herself. It was all that she could think of to do.

"Cat got your tongue today, Lily?" Magda leaned into the open car window to say good-bye.

"Kids," Lily's father replied, adjusting his rearview mirror. Heidi sat on the top step of her house, watching Lily go with narrowed eyes.

"Next time the kids get together, Heidi can come stay with us," Lily's mother told Magda. She waved as the car backed down the drive.

"Dear God, did you get a load of that sundress Magda had on?" she asked Lily's father as the car drove out of sight. Lily's mother maintained that strapless dresses were immodest.

"I don't want Heidi to come to my house," Lily said. "Please. I never want to see Heidi again."

"Oh, Lily, you disappoint me," said her mother, turning to face her in the back seat. "Your bedroom is big enough for two. You must learn to be generous, and to share. I don't want to hear another word about it. You've seen for yourself that poor Heidi hasn't had your advantages."

Lily's Ginny doll was sitting next to her, smiling in her pretty straw bonnet. She turned the little doll face down so that she could no longer see her smile. Alone in the back seat, she gripped the arm rest until her hand grew numb.

GHOST STORIES

From Monday through Friday, when the school day comes to an end at precisely 2:45 pm, Molly curtsies and says "Good afternoon, Mother Saint Marcel" along with her classmates in their identical blue jumpers and white blouses, exits her first-grade classroom, and hurries upstairs to join her sister, Betts, in the big-girls section of Notre Dame Academy. Every afternoon, the girls walk together down Church Street and along West Main. They wait at the traffic light to cross over to the Green to catch the Overlook bus for home. But lately, there has been a variation in their routine. Betts and Molly have discovered the Mattatuck Historical Society and its trove of dusty treasures.

The museum is on West Main Street, sandwiched in between the Mercy Boyd bookstore and Hamson, Mintie, Abbott's furniture emporium. It's housed in a rather forbidding red brick mansion with white iron-faux balconies and a tall white portico. They turn right and walk up four broad steps, then along a cement walk to the house set far back from the busy street. The museum is Waterbury's attic, and what's inside it is a fascinating draw.

There are Civil War uniforms that look as if they would barely fit an eighth grader, embroidered dancing shoes smaller than Molly's sturdy brown lace-up school oxfords, ivory fans, dance cards with tiny pencils attached by silken cords, pocket watches and pen knives laid out in locked glass cases, melancholy looking marble busts of dead

Waterburians, a big black buggy once used by a Waterbury doctor to make his rounds, and best of all, a wooden dollhouse.

It is the eight-room dollhouse complete with a tiny maid doll brandishing a broom that the girls like best. And so at least once a week, Betts and Molly lug their book bags up to the front door and enter the long, dim hall that leads back to the big terrazzo-floored room filled with artifacts.

It's dark inside, spooky and quiet as an empty church. And no matter what afternoon of the week the girls choose for their visit, they are invariably the only ones in the building except for the shadowy shapes of the custodian and his family who live on the other side of a locked door with a frosted-glass window panel.

"Do you think this place is haunted?" Molly whispers. She points to a white marble bust of a child. "Little Willie lives in heaven" is chiseled on its base.

"It could be," Betts says. "Maybe the ghosts miss their stuff and stop in to visit. It looks as if the people who lived in Waterbury back then had a really good time."

"But we should go now," she adds, looking at her Mickey Mouse watch. "Let's walk out so that we pass the dollhouse one last time."

That night over supper, they tell their parents about the museum.

"You should see the little white dancing shoes with embroidered flowers," Molly says. Molly likes to play dress up and imagines how she'd look in her Cinderella costume if she had those shoes to complete her princess ensemble.

"Eat your carrots, girls," Betty says. Then after a long moment of silence that someone writing a novel might describe as a reverie, Betty begins a shoe story of her own. Betts and Molly grow edgy whenever their mother begins a story. They never know if it will be a happy one or sad. Betty's childhood has been a jumble of both. The happy reminiscences are a delight to hear, but the sad ones take the spark right out of a day and, if told just before bedtime, make it hard for the girls to fall asleep.

"One year when I was just about your age, Betts, I had a blue velvet dress with a white collar," Betty begins. "My cousin Eileen passed it down to me when she outgrew it. Of course, velvet was too hot for June, but I wore it anyway. The only shoes I had were my brown school shoes, but I'd saved the quarters Uncle Dan used to give me for good report cards. There was a store on North Main Street called the Opportunity Shop that sold used clothes. And in the window was a pair of white Mary Jane shoes. They were nearly my size, and the price was right. I patched the cracks in the leather with paper that I stuck on with white shoe polish liquid. But when the polish dried, the paper fell off. How I cried," she concludes, with an odd little smile.

Molly is tearing up herself now. She is the more tenderhearted of the two sisters. Betts, though, is feeling the undercurrent of the story: guilt that she has nice shoes for best, and anger at being held responsible in some way for an event that happened so long ago that it is practically a museum story itself.

Neither of the girls understand that their mother is telling her story so that they can see how much better their own lives are. It is Betty's goal to give her girls the things she herself dreamed of when she was their age. But it's a touchy situation because although she is glad for them, Betty feels sad for the child she once was.

Rob knows better than to say it out loud, but privately he has come to think of his wife's tear provoking looks backward as *Dog of Flanders* stories, named for the book by Ouida about a boy and a dog with incredibly bad luck. Rob has never read Ouida; he has merely seen the movie, a type he calls a tear jerker, on TV late one night when he was unable to sleep.

"Hey, there are brownies for dessert, I hit the bakery on my way home from work," says Rob in an attempt to change the subject. The girls brighten, and begin to discuss their Halloween costumes. Indian summer is still in force, and Betts and Molly hope it will continue until October 31 because nothing puts a damper on a princess costume like a bulky cardigan sweater.

"We're making pumpkins for the bulletin board in our class," Molly tells them. "We cut out circles from orange construction paper and draw scary faces on them. But Mother Saint Marcel draws all the black cats." From the way she delivers this news, it is clear to everyone that Molly would rather draw the cats. Rob makes a crack about witches riding their brooms. It's a funny allusion to the nuns who teach Molly and Betts. Their habits cover them in black from head to toe except for the white headdresses that come to a point like witches' caps.

"I'll wear my Cinderella dress for trick or treat," Molly decides.

"And I'll wear the Snow White costume Grandma is making for me," says Betts.

On Sunday afternoon, they pay their weekly visit to Betty's parents.

"Tell us some spooky stories, Grandma," Molly coaxes as they gather around the kitchen table. Zora pours herself a cup of tea, adds cream, and butters her Royal Lunch milk cracker. Topping it off with a spoonful of strawberry jam, she begins.

"Ireland is a 'thin place,' you know. It's an old, old country. And the veil between the living and the souls who have passed is thin. It is thinnest on Samhain, your American Halloween. It is easier on that night for the dead to come back and have a look around." The girls look at each other and giggle. Betty and Rob roll their eyes.

"Your American jack-o'-lantern was a custom that came from Ireland, where it was most often a turnip hollowed out to hold a candle. It was a man named Jack, so the story goes, who made a deal with the devil never to go to hell. But when he got to heaven he was locked out of the pearly gates for his pact. And so Jack wanders the earth with his lantern lighted from within by a coal from hell that was tossed to him by the devil."

"Well," says Donal, "a pumpkin is a good sight more attractive than a turnip to have sitting on your front stoop for Halloween, and far easier to carve a face on, for sure."

"But how about the spooky stories?" Molly is not going to let her grandmother off the hook.

"My mother as a young woman had a nagging cough. And one evening when she was walking by the lake, a lady in black appeared to her and called her by name. Dinis, where our house is, is an island, and every night, my father locked the gates to the two bridges. There was no way the woman could have gotten on the path. But there she was. 'You are too fond of walking alone at night,' the woman told my mother. 'It would go better for you if you sought your fireside when it grows dark.' Her hand on my mother's shoulder was cold as ice. And then she disappeared before her eyes."

"Don't forget the redheaded ghost while you're at it," goads Donal. It's a story from his side of the family.

"Indeed I will not. After your grandfather Donal's mother died, the family was bereft. And no one could find her little holy medal of Saint Brigid that she'd cherished for all her life. Your grandfather's sister Katherine had a friend who was coming to tea, and as she walked along the path to their house, she was met by a ginger-haired woman who said, 'Tell your friend below in Torc Lodge that what she is seeking is close at hand. Mind her to look sharp when she is making the tea.' And there was the medal itself behind the tea caddy in a dark corner of the shelf. No one knew who the woman was, but your grandfather's mother, God rest her, had ginger colored hair."

Molly likes the idea of helpful ghosts a whole lot better than the ghost of Jack and his devil's lantern. She'd welcome a friendly ghost who could help her with multiplication.

"Is Waterbury a thin place?" she asks.

"Well it's an old place, to be sure. Hundreds of years ago when there were Indians here, it was called Mattatuck."

"Like the museum," says Molly, pleased to know how the place got its name. "So there could be ghosts around. Do you think our family ghosts are watching us?" Molly asks.

"Why not?" Zora tells her. "We carried them along with us in our memories when we came here."

There's a costume party at school after class tomorrow where the girls are allowed to dress up and feast on cinnamon sugar doughnuts and cider. Betts is standing impatiently next to Cora's Singer sewing machine while the finishing touches are put on the blue velvet vest to her costume.

"My mother sewed for me," Cora confides, "and for all my brothers and sisters."

Betts knows that her grandmother's family was a large one, and that Cora's father ran a livery stable.

"Did you ride around in buggies like the one at the Mattatuck Museum when you were small?" she asks, playing with the extra spools of thread.

Cora gets a look on her face that makes Betts sorry she has asked.

"In my family," Cora explains, "my father was Methodist and my mother was Catholic. Those of us kids who chose to be Catholic had to sneak to Mass and hide it from our father. My father found out one day that I had been to Mass, and he beat me with his buggy whip. I had to lie on my stomach in bed for weeks afterward. We had no money for medicine, and so my mother fixed my back with a poultice she made from bread soaked in milk."

Cora sighs. Betts cannot think of anything to say to this revelation. The story is awful beyond anything she could ever have imagined.

"Well, honey, I didn't mean to scare you. That happened to me a long time ago, and it could never happen to you and Molly," Cora continues. "Here, try this vest on. Your costume is all done now."

"Wow, that looks just like Snow White's dress," says Molly, who has been making a pile of the leftover scraps of material. She's been waiting for her sister so they can go up to Dave's Superette for wax lips. It's a seasonal purchase, and the bright red lips are candy flavored, so after the girls have amused themselves by imagining that the grown-ups think they are wearing lipstick, the sweet lips can be chewed and then spit out.

"Let's get those orange wax Halloween pipes too. I like the toot they make when you blow into them."

It's a pleasant diversion for Betts after Cora's story, which she has been comparing to her mother's story about those white shoes. The stories she has heard from her mother and grandmother have made it obvious to her that their pasts haunt them. And although she is a child who loves to hear about the old days, she wishes that these particular reminiscences had stayed untold.

"If you have bad memories, they are way scarier than ghosts," Betts tells her father as he tucks her into bed. "They never go away."

"Has your mother been telling you stories again?" asks Rob.

"No. This time it was Grandma," she confides.

"Honey, times are different now. And you and Molly can write brand-new stories all your own that will turn out great."

The big Halloween night arrives at last, and the girls are dressing up. Zora and Donal have driven across town to see them in their finery.

"I wonder what it would be like to live in a house like the dollhouse at the museum and have a maid like the little maid doll," Molly says.

"It would be like living in one of the big houses around the corner on the Hillside," Betts speculates. "We would be like the queen at Buckingham Palace."

Donal hears them from where he is sitting with the evening newspaper and replies, "If you two were back in those old museum days, you'd be the maids, girls, and sleeping in the drafty unheated attic of a house like the one in the museum that you think is so grand. We Irish have come a long way in America from way back then to now. Sure, we have each of us climbed higher on the shoulders of all the Irish who came before."

He waves his pipe expansively, including with the sweep of his arm their little house and backyard, the cars parked in the driveway, and Willow Street itself, as far as the eye can see. "And will continue to do so," he concludes with a flourish.

"You are very dramatic tonight," Zora tells her husband. "Maybe we should send you up to Dave's Superette for a soap box and drop you off down on the Green to preach."

Betty changes the subject before her father can think of a rejoinder.

"Well, girls, you're dressed to the nines, and you've gotten your wish about the weather. Tonight is warm enough for you to leave your sweaters at home," she says.

Cora comes down from her part of the house upstairs to see them off.

"Here, kids, I brought you some of my jewelry to wear. What good is a princess costume without some gems?" She fastens a rhinestone pendant around Molly's neck and hands Betts a big bracelet with red and blue stones shaped like gumdrops.

"I'll tag along behind you two, just for fun," Rob tells them. He'd never let his girls out after dark by themselves on a regular night, never mind one where folks are walking through the street wearing masks, but he would never tell them that and spoil their fun.

"Trick or treat," shouts Molly, trying the words on for size. "I hope we get a lot of candy tonight."

And so off they go in their gritty factory town that was built on brass, a black-haired Cinderella and a red-haired, freckled Snow White, confidently climbing the porches of the triple-decker neighborhood houses lit by 1950s versions of Jack's lantern.

Molly and Betts can't see it yet, but they are indeed writing their own stories. They are Waterbury princesses in the making, if their family has anything at all to say about it. Opportunity is one of the great things about America, their grandparents will tell you. And peering through the thin veil of All Hallows' Eve, their family ghosts nod approval. One or two of them, in fact, even cheer.

JINGLE BELLS

Molly is alone in the kitchen, which suits her purpose just fine. It's mid-December, and she is opening the door for the day in her Advent calendar. The brightly colored holiday scene of Santa in his sleigh is taped to the front of the refrigerator. The idea behind this harbinger of Christmas is to open one tiny paper door each day to see the little surprise picture inside.

Molly began the calendar on December first with number one, a door in Santa's beard. Today's door is number seventeen, a red-bowed box in Santa's backpack. The grown-ups want her to open just one each day, but Molly has other ideas. She has already opened every door she has found and then smoothed them back in place. Only door number twenty-four has proved elusive in the busy design. Molly is scrutinizing the picture for it when she hears her mother coming down the hall.

"School vacation starts tomorrow. We ought to think about going downtown to visit Santa and do some Christmas shopping."

To Molly, her mother's words are the equivalent of giving a dose of catnip to Cynthia and Priscilla, their cats. Molly's mother, Betty, had originally chosen those names for Molly and her sister. But Rob, Molly's father, thought otherwise. Betty is not one to waste anything, including a good name, so she has bestowed them instead on their pets. Downtown Waterbury at Christmastime is a wonderland of holiday decorations and stores crammed with fabulous gifts. It's a sight to make anyone's eyes glitter, never mind a kid the size of Molly.

"We'll make a day of it," Betty decides. "We'll take your sister and Grandma too."

That night after supper, Rob opens the long brown cardboard box tied with string and assembles their Christmas tree branch by branch from its complicated directions. Real trees have given way to artificial at their house, and Betty is delighted to no longer have to vacuum up falling pine needles. Their collection of Shiny Brite bulbs packed away from year to year have come down from the attic along with the strings of multicolored lights that have always managed to tangle themselves, and the angel tree topper from Woolworth's. They've had it forever, this circular confection of angel hair that frames the face of a rosy cheeked cherub with golden wings and curly blond hair. Betty bought it for her first Christmas tree as a married woman, and no matter whether their annual tree is real or artificial, this ornament remains its crowning glory.

Cora comes downstairs to watch as Rob strings the lights. Molly is unwrapping the cardboard manger and the little plaster people. It's immediately apparent that this manger has an overabundance of plaster sheep. Molly likes sheep, and in December, every time someone goes downtown, she begs for just one more to be brought home. The cats like the opened packet of manger straw. They circle the tree, cuffing at the figurines.

"Cynthia knocked Baby Jesus out of his crib," shrieks Molly. "Bad cat!"

"Well, that would never happen with Mom's setup," Rob tells them. Upstairs in Cora's part of the house, beneath her silver foil tree with the four color, revolving wheel light, lies a life-sized plaster Baby Jesus wedged firmly into Molly's doll cradle. He's swaddled in Cora's best embroidered linen tea towel, his brown glass eyes open wide. Betty suspects that he is dazed by the color wheel light that flashes blue and green, red and yellow, like a lighthouse beacon strobe with a short circuit. The baby blue lamb decals on the cradle's headboard and footboard are a handy stand in for manger sheep, Cora thinks.

Between the front windows of her living room is a red-brick patterned cardboard fireplace. There's a fluted metal ring on top of the light bulb hidden behind its cardboard logs. When the light bulb heats up, it makes the ring revolve, and the logs flicker almost like a real blaze. Cora has placed an ivory-colored plastic candelabra in each window. The flame-shaped bulbs are arranged so each candelabra has one of each color. Molly and Betts like Cora's setup so much that they always pester her to leave the decorations up year-round.

Molly knows the difference between real and pretend. Pretend is warming her hands over the cardboard fireplace's flame and feeding her dolls plastic meatloaf from her Merry Little Homemaker Kitchen Set. And as to her annual tête-à-tête with Santa, she understands that the jolly old elf waiting downtown on his gilded throne is not the real deal. He's just helping out while Santa toils at the North Pole in his workshop making toys. What has gotten Molly to thinking this year is the toys themselves. Howland-Hughes' basement Toyland, the presents Cora wraps with her "Do Not Open Until December 25" stickers, the gifts her mother buys to give to her cousins all seem at odds with the North Pole workshop story.

"Some gifts come from us, some from Santa," Betty explains.

"Why isn't there a little Santa in the manger set?" Molly asks. "They both come on Christmas Eve. Aren't Santa and Jesus friends?"

It's too early in the morning for theological discussions. Betty is busy changing beds.

"Find something to do, honey, will you?" she suggests. Molly obliges by corralling both cats in the bathroom. She has thought of a way to cure them of attacking the manger. All she needs to accomplish her mission is her mother's holy water bottle from the top of her dad's tall bureau.

"I baptize thee, Priscilla and Cynthia, in the name of the Father, Son, and the Holy Ghost," she intones as she pours water over the heads of the struggling cats.

"Wow, those are some scratches," says Rob at supper.

Next morning finds Betty and Cora and the girls dressed in their best coats and hats, waiting in front of Del aney's Drug Store for the bus downtown. In 1950s Waterbury, ladies dress to go downtown. It's a white-gloves experience, and in the Binette family, that includes little girls. Betty pulls the buzzer cord for their stop at Exchange Place, and they stroll up Bank Street. Betts recites the stores' names out loud: Worth's. Engelman's. Jones Morgan. Bedford. Howland-Hughes. The store windows are filled with red dresses and green sweaters, mounds of cotton snow, little Christmas trees, sparkly costume jewelry, and embroidered guest towels with Santa faces.

"When I talked to Santa, he already knew I'd been good this year," Molly tells them over lunch. They are seated in the Front Page Restaurant, eating spaghetti on the restaurant's thick white china plates, starched white linen napkins in their laps. It's a special treat to be lunching formally, and even Cora's joke about having to wash dishes if the bill is too high fails to dampen the girls' enthusiasm.

"Let's not forget that I need a new winter hat," Cora reminds them, steering the group down South Main Street to Jo-Belle's. *The hats here are like magic spells for women,* Betts thinks, enjoying their rainbow arrangement in groups of the same color that fade subtly from one to the next along the walls of the store like Judy Garland's signature song from her trip to Oz. Cora chooses a hat that fairly shouts Christmas, in forest green with a sprig of holly on its brim.

"I'll wear it," she tells the sales lady, handing her the old hat to be boxed.

In December, a trip downtown always includes a visit to the Green to see the big evergreen tree with colored lights and balls and the red-bowed wreaths on the Carrie Welton fountain and her bronze horse Knight's companion, the four-faced granite clock. It is Betty's father, Donal, who oversees the decorating of the Green as part of his job as a Park Department foreman, and Betty feels a sense of pride as she surveys his work.

"But, Mom, this snow is dirty. And there isn't enough for a sleigh." Reality is not matching up with Molly's Advent calendar scene, and she is beginning to worry.

"Relax. Santa still has time. And he's never missed yet," Betty tells her, juggling an armful of packages and bags.

They catch the bus home in front of Woolworth's, the store which to Betts and Molly is the Promised Land of everything desirable from parakeets to puzzles. Because it's cold out, they wait inside next to a counter heaped with a dazzling array of Christmas corsages. Betty and Cora buy silk poinsettias with glittery bows to pin on their coats while Betts opts for a bouquet of tiny Christmas ornaments with a white plastic reindeer in its center. Molly, though, goes for the plastic Santa head with a battery-powered red nose, and all the way home on the bus, she pulls the little cord on her talisman to make it glow.

"I thought I heard Santa last night," Molly tells Betts at breakfast. "I thought he was in our bathroom. But then I smelled a cigarette, and I knew it was only Dad."

"It's not the twenty-fourth yet, there's a way to go," Betts tells her. "And anyway, we haven't seen our neighbors go past our house with their tree. That's the real tip off that it's almost Christmas."

Every year without fail, a family who live somewhere up beyond their house on Willow Street walk down the hill bundled in coats and hats, scarves and boots on their journey across the river to Watertown Avenue to buy a real evergreen tree. Hours later, they return, all of them grabbing onto the branches to carry it uphill. There are seven of them, a mother and a father and five children of assorted sizes. Rob has never tried to find out where they live, he enjoys the mystery. Do they have a car? Is it some kind of ritual? Each year's speculation is as fresh and fun as ever.

"Hooray! That's the spirit," he says, peering out from a corner of the living room curtain to watch their struggle.

Molly has noticed that grown-ups talk a lot about spirit when Christmas rolls around. It includes their insistence that it is the thought behind the present that counts. Rob and Betty say this every year about the weird gifts their cousins give them, things like sweaters in a Worth's box that have really come from somewhere else, handkerchiefs as stiff as cardboard, and once, a multicolored chalk ware piggy bank with a gargoyle's face, Souvenir of Savin Rock printed on its back.

Molly knows that pretending to like these gifts is nothing at all like pretending that Cora's fireplace is real. It's another one of those mysteries from the world of grown-ups and one of those things Betty usually deals with by saying that she'll understand some day when she's older.

December 24 has arrived at last, but Molly has not yet managed to find the corresponding door in her Advent calendar. Betts helps her to discover it in a drift beneath Rudolph's hoofs. Behind the door is a tiny sleigh filled with gumdrops.

"See, that sleigh is a good sign," Betts tells her. "Keep your chin up. We could still get snow."

In the evening, Betty's parents come by to see the tree.

"The kids can hardly wait for Christmas," Rob tells them.

"Remember to say a prayer," Zora tells the girls. "Tonight is the holiest night of the year."

"And remember to make a wish," Donal adds. "It's a magical night as well."

Betts reads Molly a story, and Betty tucks her in. Rob shuts the cats in the cellar for the night.

"Sleep tight," he says. "Tomorrow's the big day."

Hours later, Molly wakes in the silent house. She can hear faint scratching from the cats on the other side of the cellar door that happens to be in her bedroom. Next to that door is the one to the side porch, a door with a big glass window. How quiet it is, she thinks. She cannot even hear the usual traffic of cars going up and down Willow Street. Molly gets out of bed and looks through the lace curtain of the window in the top half of the porch door. Heavy snow is falling. On the far side of the street, it glows orange in the light from the Hillside Tavern's neon sign. There are no cars at all to be seen.

And then she hears the faint jingle of bells and sees a sleigh. Down the center of Willow Street it comes, driven by a man who lives above them in the Overlook neighborhood and keeps a horse. The jingling bells are on his horse's harness. The snow is so deep that Molly cannot hear a hoof clop or even the swish from the runners of his sleigh. It's as deep as the snow in her Advent calendar picture, she thinks.

Molly opens the cellar door and lets the cats out.

"Look!" she says to them. But of course they don't. They twine themselves around her ankles and then jump onto her bed.

Molly watches until the sleigh is gone. She smoothes back the curtain and climbs into bed and arranges herself between the purring cats.

"Merry Christmas," she tells them and pulls the covers tight.

Is the late night snowfall magic, as Donal has suggested? Or is it an answered prayer? Molly has no idea.

She is not a philosopher yet, but years later, Molly will remember this night. By then she will be in on the secret and understand what the grown-ups meant about Christmas spirit. The secret is that it is all wrapped up together: the Santa visits for children, the manger scenes arranged beneath the trees, the Advent calendars, and even the gifts that have sometimes proved less than welcome. By then, Molly will know that it is about expecting good things to come your way. Christmas spirit is simply another way of saying hope.

CPSIA information can be obtained at www.ICGtesting.com
Printed in the USA
LVOW08s2136031013

355380LV00002B/106/P